James Douglas Jerrold Kelley

The Ship's Company and Other Sea People

James Douglas Jerrold Kelley

The Ship's Company and Other Sea People

ISBN/EAN: 9783337035235

Printed in Europe, USA, Canada, Australia, Japan

Cover: Foto ©Andreas Hilbeck / pixelio.de

More available books at **www.hansebooks.com**

THE SHIP'S COMPANY

AND

OTHER SEA PEOPLE

BY

J. D. JERROLD KELLEY
LIEUT.-COMMANDER U.S.N.

AUTHOR OF "OUR NAVY" "A DESPERATE CHANCE"
"THE QUESTION OF SHIPS" ETC.

ILLUSTRATED

NEW YORK
HARPER & BROTHERS PUBLISHERS
1897

TO

MY LITTLE DAUGHTERS

JACQUELYN, MURIEL

AND

NATHALIÈ

NOTE

—

THE " Superstitions of the Sailor" first appeared in the *Century*, the "Ship's Company" in *Scribner's Magazine*. Through the courtesy of their publishers I am enabled to reprint here the text of those sketches. A few details given in "The Spirit of Libogen" were taken from a pamphlet wherein the wreck of the *Rainier* was described.

J. D. J. K.

U. S. Battleship *Texas*,
  North Atlantic Squadron,
    October, 1896.

CONTENTS

ILLUSTRATIONS

THE SHIP'S COMPANY

THE SHIP'S COMPANY

I

WHEN the breeze is piping free and the tide is running strong none but a master-seaman may be trusted to haul out of the Liverpool Docks a great Atlantic liner. Should it be a leeward ebb, with the Mersey spinning under a flurry of squalls and snarling in angry eddies, a quick eye must mate a clear wit to make the trick a deft one. The manœuvre is always a delight to the mariner, let bo's'ns, hopelessly spliced to such traditions as topsails reefed in stays, bawl what they may about the dead days of seamanship. For here are unfolded the mysteries of the art, and here are exercised all the higher qualities of the sailor, and just as much, believe me, as in the old times when the gray piers and oozy quays were crowded to cheer our famous clippers warping in and out to the music of barbaric " chanties."

Beach-combers, shore-huggers—mere Abraham's men— will tell you the poetry is gone out of it all, and will, with much damning of their eyes, and shifting of their quids, and hitching of their tarry trousers, try to persuade you that steam has ruined the genuine sailors of story and of song. But this is mere transpontine nonsense, for above and beyond everything he who commands a ship, smoker

or sailer, as it may chance, must first of all be a seaman.
The demands of modern sea life have increased the responsibilities of the mariner, and in like measure the professional attainments required are deeper, broader, and
higher than ever before.

What the task of hauling out is you may best judge
by noting the bulk to be moved, for you can never measure
properly the enormous dimensions of these great steamers
until you see them looming in their true proportions above
the walls, and undwarfed, as they are in the open, by the
frame of sea and sky. The bulwarks tower like the walls
of a fortress; the enormous decks sweep with a sheer
knowing no broken curve; the wheel-house lifts its windows above the life-boats, swarming sternward like a school
of pilot-fish; still higher the bridges, often double-tiered,
span and grip the sturdy stanchions; and dominating all,
the elliptical funnels rake jauntily, and the yardless spars
taper till they fine away at their shining trucks into graceful coach-whips.

Shipshape and Bristol fashion, point-device in paint
and polish, the massive hull glides over the quiet waters
of the basin; you catch the sheen of gleaming brasses,
of glistening air-ports, of glazed white, and lacquered
black.   Obedient as a broken colt to the touch of the
helm, quick in response as a high-bred dog in a leash to
the guiding hawsers, she moves calmly—fit exemplar of
strength rightly tempered by even will—towards the sharp
turn where the gateway opens to the river.   Winches
chatter noisily; windlasses clink, clink musically; cap-
stans rattle with slacking cables; jets of steam dart viciously; ripples stream sternward to the bubbles of the foamless
wake; the tremulous minor, more a wail than a song, of the
docking gangs working the warps, answer the cheery "Yo
heave-ohs" of the people on shipboard; and the quick,

COALING A STEAMER

sharp orders from the bridge are echoed by high-pitched answers from the mates, watching with wary eyes everywhere. One screw turns clumsily ahead, the other circles astern, and then the ship swings easily, rounding the jagged corner in the hedge of stone with a gentleness leaving feet to spare. The bow and stern enter fairly, straight as a mason's level, the open gateway ; a strain is taken on the line leading from the quarter to the pier end ; a moment of rest, of expectation, succeeded by one of doubt, follows, and then the hail rings out blithely from the after-whaleback, " All clear, sir !"

The handle of the annunciator connected with the engine-room is jammed to " hard astern;" " ding ! ding !" rings the signal from below; the water gushes in a turbulent torrent from the outboard deliveries, the engines throb fiercely, backing with all their strength, and as the lines are rendered, slacked, eased, let go, the steamer clears the pier end with a rush, shoots far into midstream, and thus begins, wrong end foremost, her voyage westward. In the optimism of the moment the chief officer and the bo's'n grow garrulous upon the recondite subject of anchor gear ; the junior officers feel they quite deserve the good luck which makes them the hustling, bustling mates of a crack racer; and maritime Jack, still a little groggy and very much unwashed, blesses the stars that have let begin another " v'yage with an 'arf crown left of his hadvance," and the prospects of " some bloomin' American tobaccy " as soon as he is clear of the tideway.

" Not a bad job, sir," said the pilot, as the anchor takes the bottom and the ship straightens astern from her cable ; " seemed ticklish a bit for a minute when they 'eld onto the spring so long, sir ; but 'ere we are, bung up and bilge free, and with the looks of a good run, barrin' the fog per'aps, for the morrer."

The captain answers smilingly, for these two are old friends, and, what is more, the hauling out has been a joint enterprise, though the senior gets the credit, as he should. After a careful survey of the anchorage and a word with the chief officer, the captain enters his cabin and buckles down to the routine work, and there is always plenty of that awaiting him. He glows pleasurably over the handy, seamenlike-way they have left the dock, for nautical critics are plenty and keen, and if he had not taken up his berth in the river so cleverly, the ill news would have grown apace, till, with unfair variations, it reached the ears of their high nobilities—the directors.

Clear-headed, brainy, driving men are these master-mariners, and bearing patiently a responsibility that needs an iron will and a courage faltering at nothing. There is no royal road to their station, nor can willing hands make them what they must be. They cannot crawl through cabin windows, nor, for that matter, come flying in a pier-head jump through the gangway with one leg forward and the other aft. They have to fight their way over the bows, and struggle out of the ruck and smother in the fo'c's'le, by sturdy buffeting and hard knocks, by the persistent edging of stout shoulders backed by strong hearts and steady brains. If it is in them they will make their way in the end surely, and may set the course and stump to windward as they please, while others haul the weather-ear-rings and drink their grog protestingly. No; master-mariners are made, not born, and, unlike many of their brothers in the government service, have to rise by energy, pluck, merit—why enumerate them?—by a hundred qualities the world is better for owning.

Old Pepys knew how this sea-kissing goes, and tells us of his favors in this wise: "That," he writes, "which puts me in a good humor both at noon and night, is the fancy

AN OCEAN RACER OFF FOR EUROPE

that I am this day (March 13, 1669) made a captain of one
of the King's ships, Mr. Wren having sent me the Duke of
York's commission to be captain of the Jerzy, . . . which
doth give me the occasion of much mirth and may be of
some use to me." Think of that, you venturesome die-
hards, who linger all your lives at the lower sheerpole, a
post-captain by the scratch of a pen, and, above all men,
given to a lubberly scrivener and an Admiralty clerk at
that!

All these elder merchant-masters are sailor-men, some so
deep and dyed in it that if you scratch them they ooze tar,
and this briny saturation has been invariably acquired
under sail. After they have had their ships and made
many a voyage, deep-water and home, round both Capes,
east and west, wherever winds may blow and freight, the
mother of wages, may linger, they shift into steam, but always in a subordinate place. Should they stick by one
employ they are sent from ship to ship, working their way
upward until they become chief officers of the choicest
vessels in the line. Here they must wait for dead men's
shoes, or resignation, or forced retirement; but when the
chance comes they are given the command of the smaller
and less important steamers upon some subsidiary route.
Then they enter a new line of promotion, and weary are the
years of waiting, and bitter sometimes the disappointment,
before they reach the high-water mark of their service.
And with this hardly earned promotion do not come, as
in other professions, ease, comfort, and proper recompense
for duty well done, but heavier responsibilities, harder
work, and greater self-sacrifice; what is worse, and this to
the shame of the great steamship corporations, these gallant men, even at their prime, receive the most inadequate
pecuniary recognition for the burden imposed, for the mental and physical qualities exercised, for the experience

brought to bear; indeed, in no other trade or profession
is equal ability so badly paid.

The junior officers belong to all sorts and conditions of
men. Most of them have had to fight their way, though
some have parents who could well afford to pay a handsome premium for their sea education in the training-ships
stationed off the principal ports. Here they are given a
strict man-of-war tuition, though the routine of studies
and drills is, of course, modified to suit the results expected. After their apprenticeship is served they go to
sea, usually in sailing ships; and when later they choose
steam, they join as fourth or fifth officers, and enter upon
a career where their future is a hard but an assured one.
In the large employs they are encouraged to enter the
Naval Reserve, and are given time for their drills and
opportunities to qualify for the higher certificates of the
merchant service; and so much are these privileges es-
teemed that you often find on the best steamers of the
transatlantic liners one-half of the officers holding masters' certificates and junior commissions in the auxiliary
government service. Under the new regulations some of
these officers have, beside the guard-ship drill, taken a
regular tour of duty as lieutenants and sub-lieutenants on
board sea-going men-of-war, and so far this has proved a
capital plan for both services. The nationality of the
officers is British, naturally, though English and Irish pre-
dominate, the Scotch, somehow, taking more kindly to
the engineering part of the business, and the Welshmen
staying at home.

There is a well-founded belief that the deck people are
not sailormen; nor, indeed, are they in the majority of
ships—that is, not sailors in the true meaning of the word;
but, on the other hand, neither are they the mere swabbers
of decks, scrubbers of paint-work, handlers of the forward

THE BELATED PASSENGER

and after ends of trunks, or reefers of hat-boxes and travel-
ling-rugs their critics would have us believe. They belong
to a special class, not a very high one from the maritime
point of view, and are reasonably well fitted for the work
expected. This you may see at fire quarters, for example,
a drill which, in these times, is always held before the passengers come on board. As the alarm is sounded by the
rapid ringing of the ship's bell, and the commands are
hoarsely shouted along the decks, you may notice, as the
men rush to their stations, the absence of the alertness,
neatness, forehandedness which characterize the man-of-
war's men; but they are sturdy and strong and willing,
and the echoes of the orders, " Fire forward ! Main deck.
Quick's your play," have scarcely ceased before 'a dozen
hose are coupled and run out, bucket and fire-extinguisher
lines are formed, axemen and smotherers are gathered, and
hand and steam pumps started with an energy promising
a world of water. Grimy greasers and stokers rush from
below; stewards hop about as none but a steward can ; and
butchers, bakers, and electric-light-makers rally in their
appointed places, eager for work, but in the motley of Fal-
staff's draft. The captain, watch in hand, receives the reports that all the departments have assembled, and that
abundant streams have been in operation (overboard, of
course, but in the neighborhood of the fire) in blank minutes—let us say three, as a fair average—from the time the
alarm was first given. Do you wonder if he smiles and
says to his chief officer, " Very creditable, sir ; very well
done. You may secure, sir" ? Very well done it is, and
when you remember this is the first drill and many of the
hands are new, you may feel reasonably assured, should
any ordinary fire break out, that it is all Lombard Street
to a Tahiti orange it will be subdued most promptly.

The pumps stop, the hose are uncoupled, under-run, and

reeled, and, everything being secured, the ship returns to
its normal condition.   But not to rest, for there is no rest
fore and aft when a voyage is begun.   Cargo and stores
have to be hoisted out of the lighters, holds have to be
stowed, gear secured.   All day long the cargo winches
rattle, and the tackles rise and fall complainingly.   Alongside a double bank of lighters cling, and through cargo-
ports and over the rails the freight pours ceaselessly.   The
twilight deepens with stars; ashore the roar and traffic of
the busy town are hushed; the river-banks are deserted.
But under the dazzling arc-lights on shipboard, and far
into the night, toiling men and swaying bales and boxes
cast fantastic shadows on the breezy water and about the
decks and in the cavernous holds gaping unsatisfied for
the fruits of trade and barter.

THE FIRST BREAKFAST AT SEA

II

THE next day the passengers come on board, and the company's servants in the tenders and lighters gleefully escape, after banging about and muddling the baggage so mercilessly that state-room trunks yawn bruisedly in the holds, and huge chests, bursting with useless trophies of travel, lumber up your narrow quarters below—this, to the despair and tears of forlorn women who pursue the hapless purser with unrelenting fury when they learn that nothing can be unearthed until after the ship has left Queenstown, and that until then they must hopelessly shift for themselves. Steam is spluttering and flickering in little curls at the escape-pipes, the officers—every button of their best coats on duty—are at their stations, the pilot is looking wiser than ever pilot could be, and on the bridge with the impatient captain lingers a representative of the company. By-and-by, after the final instructions are given, this personage departs, and as he goes over the side the captain waves his hand in salute and gives a quiet order to the chief officer.

The wheel is shifted, the capstan reels noisily, and link by link the chain comes home. At last, after a vicious tug or two on the cable, the ground is broken, and, smothered and sputtering with cleansing water from the hose, the anchor, ring and stock, appears above the foam-streams rippling at the bow. When the catfall is hooked the ship's head swings around with graceful sheer, the engines slightly increase their speed, the wake straightens

its curves, the ensign dips in answer to salutes, and a long
blast from the whistle sonorously claims the right of channel.   Slowly, carefully, the gallant ship threads her way
among the fleet of inward and outward bound shipping;
the shores darken with moist shadows and gleam in broad
bands of fading sundrift; the lights of Birkenhead and
Liverpool glisten, blaze, twinkle, fade; the breeze blows
with spice of salt and briny coolness; the stars blink from
silvery steel into points of golden fire; and in the west,
where the splendor and warmth deepen seaward, the rolling mists, as yet resplendent in borrowed radiance, close,
broodingly, as a pall.   Sails burn in the heart of the sunset,
and long trails of smoke show where other ships have
sunk below the verge.   Finally the bar is crossed, the
lanterns on board the Northwest Light-ship flame in the
star-gemmed dusk, and with a swinging grip of the wheel
the ship is headed, at half-speed, just as night is falling,
to clear the lights of Holyhead.

Upon the bridge the pilot and the officer of the watch
peer "ahead and astern, look to windward and to lee;"
the ship slips and slides, now to port and now to starboard,
dodging the fleet intershooting this marvellous waterway
with a wealth of craft no other waters know; and the lookouts glue their eyes to their quadrants of observation, re-
porting lights and sails till the confusion would be in-
extricable, save to these steady nerves finding the pathway safely.   Down the coast the vessel runs in the
darkness, fearing naught while the stars shine and the
horizon circles clean cut above the foam-capped waters.
But as the night grows the air loses its briskness, a
light haze shrouds the sea, and the Channel fog rolls,
ghost - like, landward.   Soon only the upper stars glimmer, the moisture drips from the rigging, the iron rails
and deck-houses are damp and clammy, and the lights

LOOKOUT IN THE FORETOP

are aureoled with a dull cloud of gray and yellowish mist.

The captain takes his place upon the bridge, the engines are eased until, to the worried landsman's ears, their labored throbbing seems a devil's tattoo answering the grumbling and rumbling of the fog - whistle. Below, brawny, silent men stand at the levers, ready at an instant to stop and back, or go ahead, just as the emergency may direct. Outside the pilot-house the quartermaster strains his ears and peers nervously into the gloom, yet alert to pass any command given to the junior officer and to his messmate at the wheel. Signals from fog-whistles drift into them from other groping ships, and, at times, spectral hulls and ghostly sails loom close aboard, creeping out of the curtained night or slipping landward or seaward in search of hidden port or roadway. At regular intervals the lead is cast and the depth of water read from the scale by the unhooded glare of a lantern, and on the chart the positions given by the sounding are pricked, to guard against the tricks of treacherous currents.

And so the cheerless night drifts sadly into a wan morning, and the ship creeps warily down Channel, the weary vigil taxing the brains and bodies of those who must seek no rest because of the lives intrusted to their care.

III

AFTER the pilot has been discharged and the mails received at Queenstown, and the ship has taken her departure from the Roche Point Light-ship, everybody settles into the routine of life at sea. From the beginning watches have been kept rigorously, and the interior discipline and rules are so well-jointed that the ship seems to run herself. You hear no jarring of the cogs, feel no rough edges in the mosaic, though the government is, as it must always be, the hand of steel in the glove of velvet. The care of the ship is unremitting, even in details which if set down here would seem trivial and finicky, and every hour of the day has duties which are performed heartily and thoroughly to the foot of the letter by the officers. The number of these may vary on each line, even in different ships of the same employ, but in the largest steamers there are, besides the captain, three seniors and two juniors. The three seniors keep the watches, and each during his tour of duty has, as the captain's representative, the direct charge of the ship. The two juniors stand watch and watch—that is, four hours on duty and four hours off—with a swing at the dog-watches, and carry on, under the direction of the senior officers, the routine of the ship. Normally the officer of the watch takes his station on the forward bridge, and the junior officer sticks by the wheel-house, where, after collecting the data, he writes the log-slate hourly, and sees that the quartermaster steers the given course to a nicety. The first night

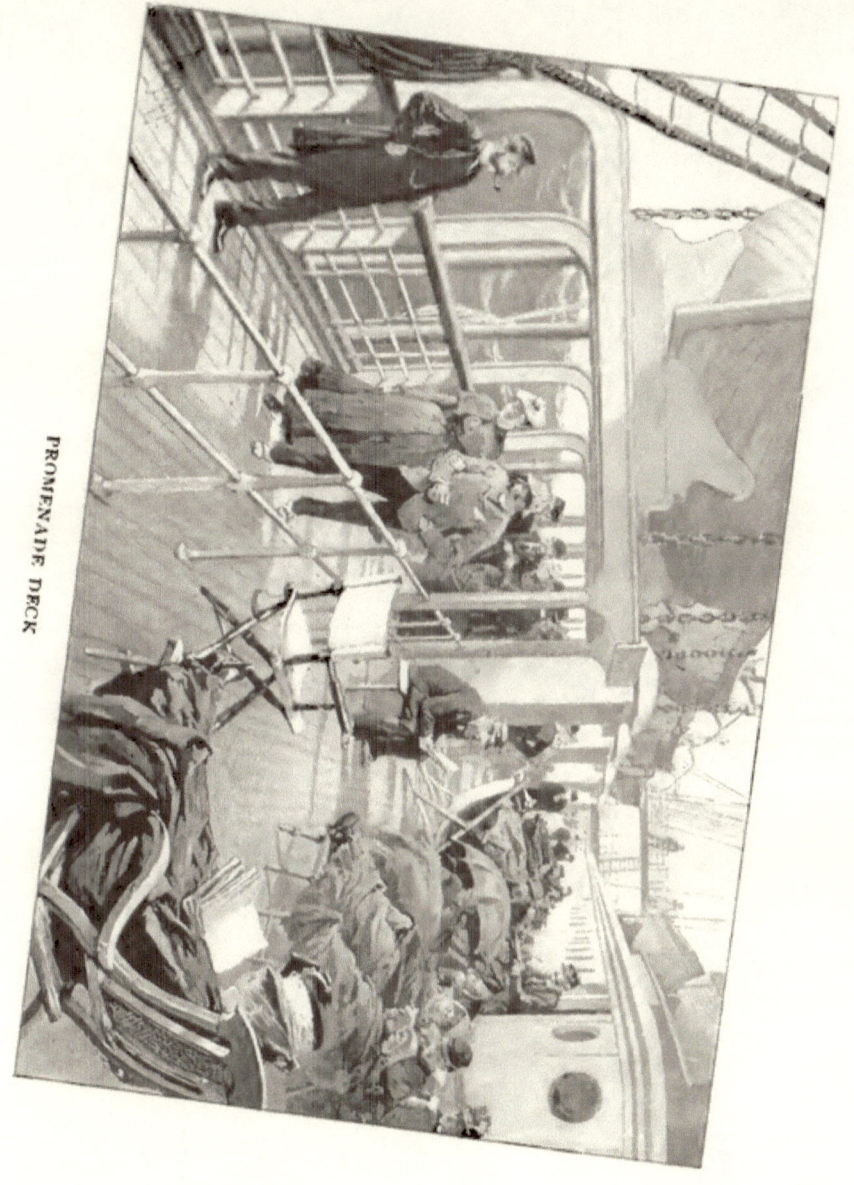

PROMENADE DECK

CALIFORNIA

at sea the starboard watch (the captain's in marine law) has the eight hours out—that is, from 8 P.M. to midnight and from 4 to 8 A.M.; and on the home voyage the mate's watch (the port) enjoys the same sweet privilege, thus sanctifying the ancient saw, which insists, under penalties dire, that the captain must take her out and the mate must take her home again.

The officers vary in their methods of keeping watch, new ships having new rules, as Simple Simon is supposed to have said when he was hustled aft to stow the jib. But to my mind, those favored in the larger steamers of the White Star Company are the best. Here the chief officer stands the watches from six to eight and from twelve to two o'clock, night and day respectively; the second officer keeps the watches from eight to ten and two to four o'clock; and the third officer those from ten to twelve and from four to six o'clock. This watch-keeping seems easy enough, even interesting and exciting, at least so I have heard not only from the casual gentle-man who worries about critically in fine weather, but from that uneasy minded shuttler who skips across the Western Ocean half a dozen times a year for no reason any sane man has yet discovered. But, dearly beloved idlers, do not deceive yourselves, getting out of bed and walking on a roof is anything but gay, even in fine weather. In stormy seasons it is such wretched work that then be mine rather to woo my bucolics, my farms and gardens, my forest glades.

Leaving out of question the responsibility, try and measure the physical misery when gales are howling, and spray is flying, and icy seas are shooting over the weather bulwarks, and the ship is slamming along, wallowing in the hollows or wriggling on zenith-seeking billows. It may be at night, when you cannot see a ship's-length ahead, and around you, threatening disaster and death, are a dozen vessels; it may be when the ice is moving and the towering bergs lie in your pathway. Then those dreadful middle watches, when, after a hard tour of duty, you are roused out of a comfortable bed, and jumped, half-awakened, into the chill and misery of the gale-blown night with every nerve and muscle strained to the breaking-point. No, it is, believe me, the hardest kind of hard work, and it so saps the body, and warps the temper, and makes the best old before their day, that no self-respecting mother will let her daughter marry a man who knows an oar from a fence-rail, if he has learned their differences— watch-keeping.

The fourth and fifth officers being young and hardy, and presumably with much to learn and suffer—for suffering somehow is considered an essential in sea training— are not supposed to need adequate rest nor sleep, and if that is not wearing on shipboard, go find me a ballad-monger to weave a rhyme for their comfort. The crew stand watch and watch; but as they can always steal a comforting nap, and have no responsibility, they know little of the mental wear and tear. The bo's'n and his mate look out for the pulling and hauling, and for the dreary singing which the " chanty " man weds to them. Their tempers are always on edge, and it is their part to buffet and bluster. These are the gentlemen you usually hear, in season and out, bellowing about decks a highly garnished sea *argot* which no one attempts to translate or deems of serious meaning. Occasionally, too, you may detect them to leeward of the houses, skylarking gloomily, in moments of forced gayety, with skulkers and sea-lawyers, "fetching them," as they describe the pastime, "a belt under the jaw," or airily promising to "knock" their "blooming 'e'ds off." These, of course, are the

STEERAGE BUNKS

vagaries of delegated authority, and should not lessen your regard for them, as they are generally good sailor-men after the heavy insular fashion. You must remember, also, they enjoy a prescriptive privilege of being most noisy, of wearing tremendous boots and very shabby clothes, and of trilling, like sea-larks, upon little silvery whistles, which are known indiscriminately as "pipes" or "calls."

In each watch there are three quartermasters, generally fine specimens of the British tar, a joy to the eye and a comfort to the soul, notably in bad weather, when they cheer you with a smile that soothes as the words they may not utter; for by a maritime fiction they are always supposed to be at the wheel, and you must not, under fear of keel-hauling, talk to them. How patronizing and sympathetic they look, what a lot they seem to know, what beautiful guernseys they wear, and with what ease they guide the mighty vessel. Before the introduction of steam steering-gear two men were always required at the wheel, and in bad weather there were four, and sometimes six, with frequent reliefs; and yet, with all this beef, many a poor fellow has been maimed for life by being tossed over the wheel-barrel or jammed by the spokes when the ship swung off with sudden lurch or broached to before the fury of the gale. To-day it requires hardly the strength of a boy to "restrain the rudder's ardent thrill," even in the heaviest blows, for the wheel in evidence is merely the purchasing end of a mechanical system that opens and shuts the valve governing the steam admitted to the steering cylinders. But be it lever or not, the sailor grasps it still with the old familiar pose, swaying it, "for the good ship's woe and the good ship's weal," with curved arm and gripping fingers as he pores over his compass and keeps its lubber's point, in fair weather or in foul, plumb on a course marked to a degree of the circle.

2

He stands a two-hours trick, and then changes places with his relief, whose station has been outside the wheel-house door.   The third quartermaster keeps his watch under the after-whaleback, ready to throw into action the hand steering-wheel when the signal is given, and as this happens seldom, his watch is apt to be a dreary one.   The pump-wells are sounded regularly by a carpenter, so that possible leaks are sure of rapid detection; and hourly every light and every corner of the ship is inspected by one of the two masters-at-arms, who constitute the police force of the ship.   They have under their special care the steerages, and a part of their duty is — as their phrase goes—"to chase" the steerage female passengers off the upper deck at dusk, and to see that they remain in their own apartment until sunrise.

First-class ships muster from twelve to fifteen men in each watch, and all of these are shipped as seamen.   Of course the majority are such only in name, though there is always a definite number of sailors among them.   Indeed, to fly the blue flag at least ten of the crew, in addition to the captain, must be enrolled in the Naval Reserve, and to be an A B there one must hand, reef, and steer deftly.   These are the people who in port stand by the ship—that is, those who take, as required by law, their discharges in Liverpool on the return voyage and continue to work on board at fixed wages per day while the ship refits and loads.   All hands, from the skipper to the scullion's mate, must ship at the beginning of each run— must "sign articles," as it is called, before a Board of Trade shipping-master.   As the law has always regarded Jack as "particularly in need of its protection, because he is particularly exposed to the wiles of sharpers," great stress is laid in these articles upon his treatment, and therefore they exhibit in detail the character of the voy-

THE GRAND SALOON

age, the wages, the quantity and quality of the food, and a dozen other particulars which evidence the safeguards thrown about these "wards of the Admiralty" by a quasi-paternal government. Jack knows all this, and be sure he stands up most boldly and assertively, at times with a great deal of unnecessary swagger and bounce, for all the articles—"his articles"—allow him.

The boatswain selects the ship's company, and the sea-birds flutter on board usually a few hours before the vessel hauls into the stream. They fly light, these Western Ocean sailors, and their kits are such as beggars would laugh at even in Ratcliffe Highway. Generally they are in debt to the Sailors' Home—they pay seventeen bob a week for their grub and lodging—and many of them just touch their advance money, as a guarantee of receipt, and then see most of it disappear, for goods fairly furnished, into the superintendent's monk-bag. But they are phi-losophers in their sad way, and are apt, if they find them-selves safely on board with a couple of shillings in their 'baccy pouches, with a pan, an extra shirt, a pannikin, a box of matches, and a bar of soap, to feel that the anchor cannot be tripped too soon, as they are equipped for an adventure anywhere, even to the "Hinjies, heast or west," as their doleful ditty announces.

Under way or at anchor they do not have many idle moments. In the middle watches the decks are scrubbed with sand and brooms and brushes, for the old, heroic days of holy-stones are over, and a hundred pounds of effort are no longer expended for an ounce of result. It might interest the passengers—especially those who look upon a sailor as so much unthinking brawn—to hear the archaic vocabulary and the emphatic dialects in which many of them are sworn at by these same mariners. In-deed, passengers are a careless, slovenly, and untidy lot, and there is scarcely a sin in the maritime decalogue of cleanliness they do not commit unthinkingly. The particularly offensive ones are soon singled out and labelled with briny offensive names ; and though they know it not, the forecastle is at times lurid with the blood-curdling anathemas launched upon them.   In the morning watch the paint-work is scrubbed, and a deft cleaner is Jackie ; and finally, when the weather permits, the brass-work— bane of every true sailor—is polished till it blinks like the rising sun in the tropics.   This scrubbing and burnishing and cleansing runs in appointed grooves through every department, and in no perfunctory way, for each day the ship is inspected thoroughly, and upon the result depends the reputation and the advancement of the subordinates.

Very formal indeed is the inspection, when, at eleven o'clock in the forenoon, the captain, accompanied by the doctor, begins his royal progress.   At the borders of each province he is received by its governor, who conducts him through its highways and its by-ways, through its lanes and shaded groves.   The purser and the chief steward are answerable for all concerning the passengers, and scrupulous and minute is the examination given to the saloons, store-rooms, pantries, kitchens, bakeries, closets, bathrooms, and to such cabins and state-rooms as may be visited.   Then follow the steerages and the "glory hole" —this last a den sacred to the discomfort of the perennially nimble, of the tip-extracting, uncannily cheerful, and sorely tried stewards.   The chief officer is responsible for the boatswain's locker, the forecastles, the upper decks, the boats, the whalebacks ; in short, above and below, wherever dirt might breed disease, no nook nor corner is omitted, not even that seething cauldron where the lungs of the ship breathe steam and her ponderous muscles drive the mighty screws.

STOKE-HOLE

IV

THE engine-rooms and stoke-holes of a great steamer are forbidden ground, are lands *taboo*, save to those special-ly asked to visit them. Here no interruptions may enter, for speed is the price of ceaseless vigilance, and horse-power spells fame and dividends. When you come to measure the region fairly, it broadens into a wonder-land ; it shapes itself into a twilight island of mysteries, into a laboratory where grimy alchemists practise black magic and white. At first all seems confusion, but when the brain has co-ordinated certain factors, harmony is wooed from discord and order emerges from chaos. It is in the beginning all noise and tangled motion, and shining steel and oily smells; then succeeds a vague sense of bars moving up and down, and down and up, with pitiless regularity; of jiggering levers, keeping time rhythmically to any stray patter you may fit to their chanting ; and, at last, the interdependence of rod grasping rod, of shooting straight lines seizing curved arms, of links limping back-ward and wriggling forward upon queer pivots, dawns upon you, and in the end you marvel at the nicety with which level, weight, and fulcrum work, opening and closing hidden mechanisms, and functioning with an exactness that dignifies the fraction of a second into an appreciable quantity. Cranks whirl and whirl and whirl incessantly, holding in moveless grip the long shafting turning the churning screws; pumps pulsate and throb with muffled beat; gauge-arms vibrate jerkingly about narrow arcs, setting their standards of performance ; and everywhere, if your ear be trained to this mechanical music, to this symphony in steam and steel, you see the officers and greasers conducting harmoniously the smoothly moving parts, as soothed with oil and caressed with waste they work without jar or friction, and despite the gales tossing the ship like a jolly-boat on the angry ocean. It is a magic domain, and one may well wonder at the genius which, piling precedent upon precedent, chains these forces and makes them labor, even on an unstable platform, as their masters will.

In the stoke-hole, however, one leaves behind the formal and mathematical, and sees the picturesque with all its dirt unvarnished, with all its din and clangor unsubdued. Under the splintering silver of the electric lamps cones of light illuminate great spaces garishly and leave others in unbroken masses of shadow. Through bulkhead doors the red and gold of the furnaces checker the reeking floor, and the tremulous roar of the caged fires dominates the sibilant sputter of the steam. Figures nearly naked, gritty and black with coal, and pasty with ashes, and soaked with sweat, come and go in the blazing light and in the half-gloom, and seem like nightmares from fantastic tales of demonology.

When the furnace doors are opened, thirsty tongues of fire gush out, blue spirals of gas spin and reel over the bubbling mass of fuel, and great sheets of flame suck half-burned carbon over the quivering fire wall into the flues. With averted heads and smoking bodies the stokers shoot their slice-bars through the melting hillocks, and twist and turn them until they undulate like serpents. The iron tools blister their hands, the roaring furnaces sear their bodies; their chests heave like those of spent swimmers, their eyes tingle in parched sockets—but work they must,

IN A FOG AND CLOSE ABOARD

there is no escape, no holiday in this maddening limbo.
Steam must be kept up, or perhaps a cruel record must be
lowered.   Facing the furnaces, the hollow upscooping of
the stoker's shovel echoes stridently on the iron floor, and
these speed-makers pile coal on coal until the fire fairly
riots, and, half-blinded, they stagger backward for a cooling
respite.   But it is only a moment at the best, for their
taskmasters watch and drive them, and the tale of furnaces
must do its stint.   The noise and uproar are deafening;
coal-trimmers trundle their barrows unceasingly from
bunker to stoke-hole, or, if the ship's motion be too great
for the wheels, carry it in baskets, and during the four
long hours there is no rest for those who labor here.

In the largest ships the engineer force numbers one
hundred and seventy men, and in vessels with double
engines these are divided into two crews with a double
allowance of officers for duty.   One engineer keeps a
watch in each fire-room, and two are stationed on each
engine-room platform.   Watches depend upon the
weather, but, as a rule, the force, officers and men, serves
four out of every twelve hours.   Should, however, the
weather be foggy or the navigation hazardous, the service
may be more onerous; for then officers stand at the
throttles with peremptory orders to do no other work.   In
relieving each other great care is taken; those going on
the platforms feeling the warmth of the bearings, examin-
ing the condition of the pins and shafting, testing the
valves, locating the position of the throttles, counting the
revolutions, and by every technical trial satisfying themselves before assuming charge that all is right.   In the
stoke-hole the same precautions are taken, the sufficiency
and saturation of the water, the temperature of the feed,
injection, and discharge, and the steam-pressure being
verified independently by both officers.

The pay of the chief engineer is said to be about £30
per month, in addition to a commission upon the saving
made in a fixed allowance of coal for a given horse-power
and an assumed speed. As some ships are economical,
this at times reaches a handsome bonus. And it is well
this pay should be large, for many of these officers have
given their best days to one employ and deserve much of
it in every way. It is said that some of the old chiefs are
the greatest travellers in the world, so far as miles covered
may count. Here, for example, is one who has made in one
line 132 round trips, or traversed 841,000 shore miles — a
distance four times that between the earth and the moon ;
and still higher is the record of another, who completed
before his retirement 154 round trips, or made in distance
over one million of statute miles.

The messes of the crew are divided into three classes :
First, that of the seamen, quartermaster, carpenter, etc. ;
secondly, that of lamp-trimmers and servants and miscel-
laneous people ; and thirdly, that of the stokers, greasers,
and trimmers. The seamen sleep and mess in the forecastle, the stewards in the glory hole, and the engineer
force in the port forecastle, or, on board the new ships, in
an apartment just forward of the stoke-hole. In all these
quarters the mess-tables trice up to the under side of the
upper deck, and the bunks are two or three tiers deep.
As a rule, the men provide their own bedding and table-
gear, the company agreeing to give good food in plenty,
but nothing more. This seems shabby, even if in these
degenerate days we need not hope to find a ship's husband
like Sir Francis Drake, who not only " procured a complete
set of silver for the table, and furnished the cook-room
with many vessels of the same metal, but engaged several
musicians to accompany them." I am afraid the only
music you will hear in these dreary quarters is the shout

TAKING AN OBSERVATION

when the "snipes," as my lieges the stokers call the coal-
trimmers, rush in at eight in the evening with the high
feast known as *the black pan.* This olla podrida consists of
the remains of the saloon dinner, and is always saved for
the watch by the cooks and bakers in payment for the
coal hoisted for the kitchens and galleys. It is a grewsome feast, as one may well imagine, but it is the supreme
luxury in the sea life of the stoker and his pals, and is
enjoyed point, blade, and hilt.

Thrown together as the people are for a run only, you
find little of the messmate kinship which is so strong in
longer voyages among seafaring men. Should any one of
them become unfit for work through sickness (and very ill
he must be when the doctor excuses him from duty), his
mates, the one he should have relieved and the other who
would have relieved him, each stand two hours of his
watch. But as the attendant abuse is great, and the
curses are loud and deep and bitterly personal, no one,
save a very hard case, will leave his work as long as he can
stand up to it. As for kindness and usefulness, or any
other saving grace, they are unknown ; are, in the grim
pessimism of this iron trade, never expected. It is a hard,
hard life, measured by decent standards, and, *messieurs,*
when you stray below, and, as tradition demands, they
"chalk you"—ring you about with the mystic circle
which means drink-money—be sure the ransom is not
niggard, be certain that with it you lend them from your
brighter world the sunshine of a cheery greeting, the tonic
of a friendly smile.

For, God help them ! they need it always.

V

THE inspection is finished a little after seven bells, and one by one the officers straggle on deck with their sextants. Should it be a fine day, with moderate weather, the noon observation for latitude is a simple one and is always sought; though, in the open, these people running in regular lanes can place great dependence on their engine revolutions, their well-tried compasses, and, if the speed is not excessive, upon their taffrail logs. When the sun crosses the meridian twelve o'clock is reported, and "eight bells are made" by the captain, for no lesser personage dare trifle with the astronomical proprieties hedging about this occult ceremony. The ship's time, however, remains unaltered, until the clocks are corrected at midnight from calculations based upon the chronometer ticking stolidly in the chart-room. In the sweep of modern progress, the sacred rite of heaving the log is no longer celebrated. The speed is now too great for that rough-and-ready hit-or-miss at distance run; and with its disuse, worse luck, a fund of old-time pleasant raillery has been eclipsed. "How fast are you going, my man?" was an invariable question of the inevitable, curious passenger to the Jackie walking away with the dripping log-line. "Fourteen and a Dutchman, sir," would be his answer, or, if again pressed, "Thirteen and a marine," he would reply gravely, to the joy of his grinning shipmates and to the mystification of the questioner. But now no longer does the reel turn swift, no longer does the

DINNER

sand run dry, no more the chip dances on the waves or tugging line strain brawny muscles. To-day the speed is read off from a little cylinder which twists its dials on the weather rail.

The observations are worked out independently by the chief and second officers, and the former submits his results to the captain. Of course these calculations cannot have the exactness of astronomical work ashore, and luckily on the high sea this is not needed. On the contrary, over-precision often multiplies the error, and it is good navigation if you can say with assurance that the ship is anywhere within an enclosing circle five miles in diameter. Of course it is widely different when a vessel is running in for the land or coasting, for then the soundings, the cross-bearings of well-known marks, and the contour lines enable the position to be marked with very great accuracy.

The noon position of the ship is—next to dinner—the great event of the day, and many are the pools and bets made on the figures of the run; not only as to the distance, but as to the probable time of arrival. For if the voyage be now half over, the novelty of sea life is at low ebb, and the passengers, save a few irrepressible spirits, have lapsed into a gentle melancholy induced by the monotony of water, water, water everywhere. They are tired of the sea, of the ship, of the cooking, of each other, in short, of everything, and are anxious only to arrive. They have divided and subdivided, and differentiated into cliques, and have nursed dislikes, usually founded on feminine fancies, until these have become mortal antipathies. In a perfunctory way they follow a routine which finally drags a lengthening chain. They get up and pitchfork on their clothes, and eat, lounge about, doze, muffled to the eyes, in lashed steamer-chairs, read languidly, gossip gleefully, and eat, and eat, and eat, and then, wearied to bitter boredom, go to bed again. The men drink more than is good for them—indeed, some of them have an eager and a nipping air all day long; and as for smoking, why, those who can are blowing moist and soggy weeds and fondling explosive pipes from morn till dewy eve. The noisy ones—and what nuisances they are with their aggressively robust health and unfailing cheerfulness —play all manner of stupid sea games, horse-billiards, quoits, and shuffle-board, and sometimes venture upon such silly practical joking that you wish a sea would wash them overboard.

No one sees much of the ship's officers, except perhaps the ubiquitous purser and the amiable doctor, and how these two, harried and beset as they are by a hundred cares, by the little miseries of other people, can present an unfailing front of courtesy, can go smilingly and cheerily about their duties, is one of the sea mysteries yet unsolved. Blow high or low, and in fair weather or foul, they are ever the same, bright, beaming, optimistic, en- couraging—"fresh as a garden rose, soothing as an upland wind"—and knowing the strain put upon you by silly men and fretful women, gentlemen, I salute you, *chapeau bas!*

In the beginning there was a struggle for seats at the captain's table, and heartburnings are not unknown to those who sit a little lower at the feast. But these are not the wise or wary ones, not the tough and devilish sly travellers who know their bread will be best buttered by rallying around the purser or forming in hollow squares about the shrine where the doctor sits enthroned. The captain's duties permit him to go below rarely save at dinner-time, and as for the other officers, they live and mess alone, and are as cloistered, so far as the passengers count, as the preaching friars of Saint Dominic.

ROUGH WEATHER

Once in every voyage boat drill is held, and sadly insufficient for the people on board is this same boat equipment. But the drill is usually a passably fair one, and, given time, adequate perhaps for any demands made upon the ship by outside distress. And let it be added that never yet, when the word has been given, have those gallant men who walk their watches so quietly and so uncomplainingly, been known to fail if succor were needed by helpless mariners. It may be that death stares them in the face, that their mission may be another tragedy, but they never question. Honor to them and to all the unrecorded heroes, the uncrowned martyrs of that western passage. Who may number them? who tell their gallant deeds? True descendants are they of those "who first went out across the unknown seas, fighting, discovering, colonizing, and graving out channels through which the commerce and enterprise of England have flowed out over all the world."

You may count, as a rule, upon disagreeable weather in the Western Ocean, and this tries the temper of people who might be saints ashore; and, say what you will, even under the most promising environments, women are out of place on shipboard. However, if the days are reasonably pleasant as the voyage shortens, the monotony becomes so much a habit as to be no longer a burden. The little animosities which seemed eternal disappear, and friendships are made, and toward the end all but the hardened cases, the mental dyspeptics, or those to whom sea-sickness is a serious matter, really enjoy the voyage.

The tonic of the sea air courses like an elixir in the blood; young women begin to take notice, and you hear rippling laughter, and see, in place of gloom, the sunshine of happy smiles. This is usually the season when the concert is given, and the uneasy spirits of the ship exploit

the talent they have discovered. Usually there are a
dozen mild rows over this performance, and invariably a
great dispute as to the distribution of the money. This is
apt to divide the ship temporarily into two warring camps,
but in the end the ship's officers have their way, and the
American dollars jingle musically in English contribution
boxes. More or less jollity is always afloat in the smoking-
room, for here eddy the flotsam and jetsam of the ship.
Here, too, the speculative gentlemen, their friends and
lambs, usually play cards from early forenoon till the lights
are turned out. There is not much growling among these
industrious workmen, though at times when Jack pots go
one way, and the kitty or widow is large enough to make
the losers boisterously assertive, you may hear sharp words
over the reckoning. As for those who enjoy a quiet
rubber, they must find another retreat; the smoking-room
is ruled by the gods of clamor.

And so the last days are apt to rush along pleasantly
enough; the solitude cheered by passing vessels and the
lazy routine of the ship enlivened by congenial compan-
ionships newly found. The edge of the Grand Banks is
skirted happily without injury to the daring fishermen;
the Georges are rounded, and then, oh, happy hour for
many homesick hearts! the cry " Sail ho !" rings out with
a newer meaning, and a graceful pilot-boat wings toward
them like the fabled sea-bird. How they greet the bluff
pilot, coming as he does to their seeming helplessness out
of the known and the enduring. The speculative passengers find an especial interest in the incident, for no
pools are more favored than those made on the number of
the boat, no bets more frequent than whether the figures
are odd or even. After the assurance that the " pilot is
really on board " over-sanguine and inexperienced females
madly rush below and pack their trunks and get ready for

PILOT BOARDING A STEAMER

an immediate shore-flitting, afraid, perhaps, they will be late; but there is many and many a tossing mile yet to steam ere the services of the adventurous pilot will be needed.

Still, a new delight possesses everybody, and it grows as the hours fly, until at last, it may be at night, perhaps, some one bursts breathlessly into the crowded smoking-room or bar, and cries exultingly: " There she is, Fire Island Light, right over the starboard bow !" Joyous faces gather near the crowded bulwarks, and eager eyes hail with gladness the shining petals of that rose of flame which blossoms unfailingly above the shoaling waters; for the voyage is nearly over, and the morrow means to some the marvels of an unknown land, to others, luckiest and happiest of all, home and dear ones.

THE SQUADRON CRUISE

THE SQUADRON CRUISE

I

To get the marrow out of yachting requires leisure, patience, and money. In boats there is a wide liberty of choice, and type and rig are always a question of intention. An ideal cruiser may be built, and, so far as the inexact science of naval architecture permits, a capital racer be designed, but the best qualities of both can never be combined, because of the compromises required by extreme development in any single direction.

Then, too, the environment of the yachtsman limits his liberty as much, perhaps, as his theory of the sport. He may elect to cruise or to race; to take his outing within our peaceful waters or off stormier coasts. He may be bitten by the tarantula of matches, be possessed of the fury of mug-hunting. There are owners, generally elder brethren of the guild, who distil their sailing elixir from sedate potterings coastwise. These are eager only for fine weather, night anchorages, and capable stewards. These · are content to skim blue waters peacefully, and to gain occasional cups or sweepstakes in amiable contests with similar easy-going ships. Others struggle till they bleed by the seven veins for prizes and squadron trophies; and when the cruise is done, and the mugs have escaped them, they diminish their rigs from clew to earing, and for the fag-end of the season seek consolation in waters eastward.

But whatever you may do, be sure that the best possibilities of yachting are found mainly in such boats of a good size as have not had their safety and comfort sacrificed to speed. For all-around pleasure the usual small boat is no better than a harness cask; but if the yachtsman has had a sea training, or has been long enough on the water to accept its moods, its wiles, and tricks with philosophy, he can get out of small, deep boats a world of profitable enjoyment. For these unite comfort, safety, and speed in a high degree, and when properly handled return a very great deal for the money expended.

If, however, the yachtsman pins his faith to a type which is more nearly American in essential ideas, he will find that a well-found boat costs much to build, more to keep going, and, when no longer wanted, sells for a song. The leisure of the man really fond of the water and embarked for pleasure ought to be unvexed, abundant; a holiday free from discordant interruptions, independent of wind and tide, careless of calm and current drifting him miles to leeward of his port. His patience must smile life's little miseries afloat into the limbo of indifference; must be such as blinks at impositions with the blindness of angels. And the money! Ah! the coin of the realm. Put money in your purse, sweet sirs; put money in your purse when you go a-yachting. It cannot be little nor doled grudgingly; it may be like the purse of Fortunatus, and flow as freely as the waters of the salt sea.

A horse may or may not eat his head off in a year, but, like the torch-bearing Arab and his brothers, a yacht can bolt itself from truck to keelson, from knight-head to stern-post, in a season. Time happily was when regattas and cruises were shared by men able to spend every sum-

THE OWNER AND HIS FRIEND

mer a far-reaching thousand dollars or two, but those were the days of wampum and civic crudeness, and such chances linger no more in the nests of yachting years.

There are men of idleness, wise and wary in experience, with treasuries not so deep as a well nor so wide as a church door, who sail the year around, or, in their hardest luck, for many days in every season. But these are the masters, the illuminati; theirs is genius, and this a gift coming by the light of nature, and with its magic sealed save to the adept.

I wonder how they do it—so well, so gracefully!

Others, mainly of the cat-boat and jib-and-mainsail class, who have neither time nor coin to spare, steal afloat on rare holidays, whitening our bays and rivers with shining sails. Plate and pewter trophies of victory burden their sideboards; they enter and capsize in every regatta from the Capes of Delaware to Portland Bay; and no Admiral of the Blue dares on occasion to be half so nautical in garb and lingo as these are normally. But, scoff as they may, theirs are not the joys, theirs are the kicks and not the ha'pence of the sport.

Their fun, riotous in sunshine and soldiers' breezes, is grewsome when dreary and dripping days send their little crafts shivering shoreward with hatches clapped to tightly. They know the conveniences of a howling cowboy; they endure trials under which St. Simon of the Pillar succumbed. The sunshine must be hoarded till its sweetness is extracted to the latest sip; their calendars are white or black as waters are smooth or rough. If their pleasure be taken in a single-hander they are unhappy, for, at the best, it is dull work sailing alone; and if they are gregarious, what could be more dispiriting than cruising with a free company, knowing no leader, living in quarters as crowded and bilgy as a slaver's hold, and at the bitter end bickering like buccaneers over the shot and reckoning?

From the beginning yachting has been a diversion of those known favorably by bankers, and "favored with the friendship of the nobility and gentry." Of course, like other amusements, it has grown more expensive year by year, and more is the pity of it. In England it has always found favor with the very rich, from the days when Phineas Pett, master designer, filched the idea from Holland, and built, in 1604, for Henry, Prince of Wales, the first recorded pleasure craft. Pepys and Evelyn tell how royalty encouraged it. "By water to Woolwich," writes the former, "and saw the yacht lately built with the help of Commissioner Pett. . . . Set out from Greenwich with the little Dutch *Bezan* to try for the mastery, and before they got to Woolwich the Dutch beat them half a mile; and I hear this afternoon on coming home, it got before three miles, which all our people are glad of." This *Bezan* was the *Mary*, a yacht given to King Charles by the Dutch East India Company. Evelyn describes the first Corinthian race, a match for £100, between the King and his brother, the sailor, Duke of York. The course was from Greenwich to Gravesend, and the King "lost it going, but saved stakes returning, sometimes steering himself, his Majesty being aboard with divers noble persons and lords." Mark this — the noble company. *That* has not changed at any rate. Like the King, an owner never lacks for divers persons, lords or commoners. Even in our days no one need be lonesome on a yacht.

And this is fortunate; otherwise what a world of engaging qualities would moulder for lack of fruitful gardening, for dearth of sunshine, dew, and air! A hundred varied but excellent motives, called into activity by this

A CORINTHIAN CREW HAULING AFT THE MAIN-SHEET

giving and taking of hospitality, expand the owner's heart, crowd his quarters, and encourage into lively growth the accomplishments of his guests. What an audience for the story-teller! What a fallow field for the chestnut planter, for the banjo picker, for the singer who is high proof against night air, fogs, encores, and commissariat!

What a lucky dog is the friend of an owner! How ornamental or uselessly useful he can be! And luckiest of all, *the* favored one, ready with quips and quaint fancies, who hears the gentleman paying the rent say, with effusion: " There, old man, there is your card clinched over the best state-room door! Whenever you sail with me, out goes the occupant, whoever he may be—and we'll all have a drink on it now. Steward, bring glasses!" Ah! benign indeed is the star of such a being, and I do not know but I had better begin again, and say that the choicest possibilities of yachting are given only to those who can bring to it leisure, patience, and some other fellow's boat and money.

II

THE yachting season opens up on Decoration Day, and the regattas run well into June. Mindless of the uncertain winds and balmy skies of this month, the clubs urge their cracks into a spin, or quite as often leave them to drift around an inside course. The events are always interesting at the start, and have a sentimental value because each year introduces the rosebud craft, if I may borrow this poetic adjective from the choniclers of society small-beer. Enthusiastic friends of both sexes crowd the club steamers to the guards, and should the race be finished between luncheon and dinner, applaud the victors with joy as boundless and with hearts as free as the blue sea so carefully avoided.

After this dress parade is over, nothing official bothers the yachtsman, and he may steam or sail or lie at anchor, as his fancy wills. But as soon as late July and early August shut down the throttle of trade, and give ease for repairs and oiling the machinery of money-spinning, the clubs are summoned to a rendezvous for the annual cruise. This meeting is always appointed for some central harbor, the clubs about New York usually selecting one of the pleasant roadsteads indenting the Long Island or Connecticut shores.

When the day comes, the yachts already assembled await eagerly the arrival of the Commodore, for custom demands that he should find his squadron gathered. Just before sunset, rarely later, the black hull with the blue flag at the

main rounds the ledge buoy at the river's mouth, and
steams sturdily for the anchorage. Off the light-house she
is slowed, later stopped, then backed; and just as stern-
board is making the engines wheeze into silence, the
anchor with sullen plunge drops bodily, shank and ring,
from the cathead, and the water about the forefoot whitens
into spray and foam. Slowly she slips astern in spite of
the rattling and clinking of her straightening chain; and
at last brings up with a jerk that tautens the cable viciously
from shackle to hawse-pipe. The lower booms swing out
to the cheery piping of a bo's'n's whistle, and are squared,
lift and guy, with a nicety dividing west and sou'west sides;
a jet of smoke darts from the starboard gun-port, a resounding echo grumbles hillward, and as the Commodore
makes his finest bow from the bridge, the world may know
the tryst has been kept, and the mating of flag and pennant has been saluted decorously.

Then the expected, the inevitable, follows. It is a sul-
phurous, brain-cracking pandemonium.

Yachts, big and little, steamers, schooners, sloops, and
cutters bang to starboard and to port; bang ahead, to
windward and to lee, and with a welcoming fusillade that
drives all the joy out of life, all the peace from sea and
shore. Smoke, choking fumes, the misery of villanous
saltpetre, of heart-breaking clamor, are everywhere. Powder clouds, flame-slitted, roll upon the water, and soar till
a silvery eclipse shuts out the hulls and spars, and even
"the topmost truck, where flew the burgee with the field
of blue," as the fo'c's'le poet tunefully sings. The green
shores, the river, the beaconed ledges and buoyed reefs,
the light-house on the spit, the summer homes, the dull,
dead seaport, all slip helplessly into the Powder Fog, and
for a time are lost on a Grand Bank of its making.

After the Commodore returns the salute with his port

gun, the vapor blows down the wind, and the hulls—mainly black and white, with always a touch of gold and the sheen of bright work somewhere—emerge from the gray after-haze. The ensigns flap into distinctness of color, the tracery of gear and spars is silhouetted against the greenery ashore, and the squadron drifts against the blue above, and floats double—swan and shadow—in the blue below.

You may count this gentleman's park of masts intershot with steamers' funnels until your eyes and fingers can no longer reckon, and you will not enumerate the half of it. You will, perhaps, be lost in profitable reverie when you come to measure what these hundred and odd boats represent, for they are the files of a small battalion in the army of workers that have conquered the material. They mean fruitful energy, luck nearly always, often victory over tremendous odds. Here are ripened the luxuries which we all think we deserve as well as our neighbor, and could enjoy so much better. Here is the outward evidence of ease and freedom, of plenty in a world where most of us have to fight so hard for other things than cakes and ale and ginger hot i' the mouth too.

It is the luxury of life open to the admeasurement of all, and with the merit that, though it may be hedged in, it cannot be debased by money. Amateurs must always control it; it will ever be the one sport into which professionalism has not been injected as the main interest and purpose. And this is because it comes from the sea. With all its exclusiveness to touch, it is the least selfish of amusements. No jealous framing hides the picture; no surly keeper guards the wicket. It lies before you freely and openly as if ordered for your pleasure; it can be seen without asking. For long distances up and down the reaches of the river the spars can be traced, and near the centre, off the landing, the flag-ship shepherds her flock.

A LITTLE FISHING

From the upper harbor to the ugly turn at the reef near the haven's mouth the squadron rides to the tide in no order save such as prudence demands; and in the flooding sunlight you can mark its outer limits, the Soundward van, guarded by the shining hull of a famous steamer.

Clear of the channelway the royal masts of a sloop of war tower above the loftiest of the pleasure craft, and just before sunset her bugles sound the call for retreat. The yachtsmen stand by ensigns and stay lanterns, and as the clear notes ring musically, flags sink slowly and white lights glimmer like glowworms against the rosy skies. The breeze cools the sun-warm, sweet-scented air; the shadows deepen in the greenery of the land; and the tide, shooting arrowwise from cable and cut-water, ripples aft with a song to the streaming wake. There is a promise of festivity in the twilight; smoke curls from forecastle stove and galley funnel; echoes of quickening hospitality ebb and flow from neighboring boats; visits are made and invitations are shouted over the water; until, at last, the poetry of the enfolding dusk quiets the merriment of the visiting yachtsmen.

But the silence is broken by a cheering hail from below:

"On deck there! you sailor-men! alleged and otherwise! How would a cocktail, only one, only a little one —how would it go, just now?"

How would it go? The chorus is unanimous.

In smooth water on shipboard you are always hungry, if not thirsty, for every condition sharpens the edge of expectant appetite. Under the awning, or from deck or cockpit, you see cabins shining in the wide circle of shaded lamps, and tables gleaming with glass and silver. Nimble stewards back and fill from galley to pantry, and tack and wear from starboard to port, and from port to sherry, or to something else; and with ears attuned to liquid harmonies, you hear from mysterious recesses the "cloop" of corks yielding their treasures with expiring song.

It is a brave, a bustling hour, for lamps are trimmed and boards are spread; and as the after-glow leaves the river and the skies are a glory of stars, the fleet is mantled in silence, and agleam with lights streaming from deck-house windows and open-air ports. If you are wise, you are merry with the promise of the moment, and, rejoicing in these signs and portents of the feast, resolve to go ashore no more.

SEVEN BELLS—COCKTAILS

III

ONE of the questions asked most frequently, usually out of pure idleness, is, "What does all this cost?" The answer is necessarily indirect and vague. In the beginning of things a yacht is always an expression of its owner's individuality, a witness to his opportunities. Between any two boats, even those equipped and sailed under similar possibilities, sharper contrasts exist than within the same owners' homes ashore. The element of cost must always, therefore, be an individual question; and the problem can be solved only by an appeal in each instance to the one person who is in possession of the facts. An outsider may hit or miss all around it, hitting perhaps rather closely in the widely divergent cases of boats sailed either with an absurd bung-and-spigot lavishness or with a farcical meanness. The first cost of a craft, the number of her crew; their wages, rations, and uniforms; the probable repairs, insurance, interest, and annual depreciation; the length of the season—all these factors may be treated intelligently. But who can weigh the personal elements, the temperament of the owner, his scale of living, the extent of his hospitality, the honesty of his servants, the watchfulness exercised, the work to be done—for racing costs more than cruising?

Here at anchor, for example, are two steamers, one a family ship, the other the crusier for a bachelor; both belong to the very highest class, A 1, first rate, well found, and fit for service in any navigable waters of the world.

The annual expenditures are very great, but the returns in comfort and amusement must justify them, for both boats are nearly always in commission.

The former has on deck three steel houses, teak-sheathed and mahogany-lined; in the forward one is a smoking-room, furnished with divans and tables, and so framed with plate-glass windows as to give an uninterrupted view ahead and on each beam. Abaft this are a chart-room and cabin kitchen, between which a vestibule and carved oak stairway lead below to the saloon and owner's quarters. The saloon is thirty-one feet wide and eighteen long; its floor is a mosaic of hard-woods, and the sides and ceiling are wainscoted and panelled with polished native woods, and finished in an enamel of white and gold. A carved mantel and fireplace face the entrance; overhead is a domed skylight; and in every available spot rugs, tapestries, pictures, cabinets, lamps, the hundred and one accessories of the most opulent homes, accentuate the warmth of color. Forward of this are eight state-rooms, built of cherry and walnut picked out in white and gold, and furnished with rugs and tapestries. Each has a hand-carved bed, dressing-table, chiffonnier, and wardrobe. In the floor a porcelain bath is let so deftly that the trap can scarcely be seen even when the rug is removed. In a corner a Scotch-marble basin is supplied with hot, cold, and salt water. Electric bells and incandescent lamps are at command, and through a wide-rimmed, polished air port a cheering measure of sea and sky is secured. A nursery nineteen feet long, eleven in width, completes the owner's special quarters. In this well-ventilated anomaly on shipboard a child's berth is built four feet from the floor. Beneath this, sliding snugly out-board in the daytime, is a nurse's bed; this can be extended to such a distance at night that should

NAIADS

the child be thrown out in bad weather by a lurch or roll, it will land safely on the mattress below or upon its attendant, who is presumably a cheerfully elastic person.

A scuttle in the pantry gives access to the store-rooms, wet and dry, to the ice locker, and to the apparatus for making artificial ice. A separate stairway connects the pantry with the kitchen above, which may thus be called "hygienic," as it is in every sense on the roof. These quarters, with the linen closets, clothes lockers, toilet-rooms, and a glass armory, occupy the space in the centre of the ship between the first water-tight compartment, where the crew live in downy ease, and the forward bulkhead of the boiler-room, where the coal-heavers and firemen smoke surreptitiously the soothing but penetrating black 'baccy. A passageway, recessed and upholstered at one point to give a view of the machinery, leads aft to a library fitted and furnished as luxuriously as the saloon. Abaft this are seven state-rooms for guests, no whit less perfectly appointed than those of the family, and with a separate companion-way. In the after-house on deck is a ladies' saloon and a fair-weather state-room for the owner, and from it a stairway leads to the library. This vessel cruises at home and abroad, and carries a crew of fifty. Her cost was three hundred thousand dollars, and the annual expenditure amounts to one hundred thousand.

In the second steamer, the smoking-room is of oak, the wainscoting and ceiling are built of artistically panelled mahogany, and the furniture is upholstered in olive-green plush. Heavy plate-glass windows give a view half-way around the horizon, and if any one knows a better place to smoke a cigar at anchor or under way, let him stand and deliver. Abaft this is the chart-room, flanked by a carved stairway leading below. In the saloon, brass

chandeliers, decorated in the Persian style, hang clear
of a skylight colored in harmony with the general treatment. The mantel, panelled in carved old English oak,
is supported by dolphins, and the nickel grate is fitted
in a recess tiled with blue and silver. The bevelled-glass
doors of the bookcases flame with prismatic colors; the
wainscoting is sheathed with mahogany and cherry, and
the walls are of dark-blue lincrusta, figured into squares,
and ornamented and intertwined by golden thistles. The
ceiling is tinted ocean blue, with all manner of odd marine
animals "swimming about in this immovable sea with
trailing golden wakes," as the reporter from whom I borrow
the description joyfully records. Every nook and corner
is crowded with the artistic fruits of taste, travel, and
money. A carved cherry bedstead, chiffonier, wardrobe,
and wash-stand form the permanent furniture of the
owner's room; its walls are covered with flowered chintz,
and the door is panelled and fitted with mirrors. In the
ladies' saloon forward the wainscoting is moulded into
squares, and the sides are draped with cretonne; bevelled
mirrors are let into the doors and cabinets; and there are
crystal chandeliers in bronze framings, and brass side lamps
fitted for use with oil or electricity. The floor is laid in
highly polished hard-woods, and in an angle stands an
upright piano, framed and carved in harmony with the
other furniture of the room. The crew have comfortable
quarters forward, number over fifty, and are given employment the year round.

These slight sketches of the living quarters faintly
outline the luxury of such vessels, and though the larger
ships offer better possibilities, yet in all yachts it is found
to a definite degree. No very vivid imagination is required to picture what the living up to this particular
blue china must cost, though it can be described in a

VISITING

general way only, and from the data open to everybody. One authority in a position to know states that for a season of five months a steam-launch forty to fifty feet in length imposes an outlay of $2500; a steamer from seventy-five to a hundred feet in length will cost about $10,000, and one slightly larger, with flush decks, not less than $11,000. In the big steamers, with crews varying from thirty to fifty men, the monthly expenditure varies from $6000 to $12,000; and in two yachts of this kind described by another writer, who gave the details, the annual cost was figured at $150,000 each; and in an isolated instance where a steamer made the voyage around the world the expense for the five months' cruise was said to have been something over $50,000. Leaving these extreme cases, and taking as a fair basis steamers belonging to the class which includes vessels measuring from seventy-five to one hundred feet, we get the following fixed charges: monthly wages, fireman, cook, steward, three deck hands, engineer, and pilot, $380; coal, $200; repairs, deck stores, engine-room supplies, uniforms, $540; and mess, $380; commissioning and laying up, $2500; total for five months, $10,000. If to this be added what it costs for the cabin outfit, without the delusion that you are saving so much on your shore expenses—for in the long-run you never do—it will be seen that it costs a pretty penny for the sport.

There is not a very great difference, save for coal, in the running expenses of a steamer and a sailing craft. Indeed, on similar displacements, the larger schooners often cost more to keep up. So far as the smaller schooners and sloops go, it is an axiom that you always spend more than you have allowed. One owner of a sloop, whose experience is not exceptional, confesses that when he had built his ship for $10,000 he hoped to get

4

her into the water for $5000 more, but by the time sails were bent and he was ready to cruise, his total expenditures had reached $16,500. His first season cost him $8000 more; but from his own accounts it is easy to see the cabin was run carelessly, and too lavishly for comfort. In the next year he had his yacht hauled out by the ship-builder for an examination, and though the sailing-master had taken good care of her, his bill for a spike here and a graving piece there was nearly $1000. A new mainsail and other sail-making jobs cost another $1000, and before he got the rigger out of the boat there was a hand-spike and serving-mallet account of $200. Altogether he found his running expenses for the second season, in a boat under sixty feet on the water-line, averaged $50 per day, and it must be added that he was not a Johnny Raw.

INTERVIEWING THE COOK

IV

BUT be the expense what it may, black care is thrown
to the cats, and no death's-head jibbers and grins at any
feast to-night. The worries of the day are whistled down
the wind, and all hands are too busy with the play of
knife and fork, with the music of clinking cup to heed
the reckoning. These dinners always have a zest of their
own, a flavor of the unusual, due to the novelty of the
scene, the appetite, and the unconfined joy of the loose
sailor togs, for it is heresy to doff these save when dining
with the Commodore, or when it is tacitly understood to
be required on board a few of the larger boats. The
proverb that racing men never dress for dinner is found
so profitable by the cruisers as to make the custom
practically general.

When you go on deck for the coffee and cigars and
the *chasse*, which, as Voltaire said of Admiral Byng's
shooting, is to encourage the others, lights are twinkling
everywhere. As soon as the darkness has fully shrouded
the water, the sky is suddenly aflare with a signal rocket,
and in a moment Roman candles and port-fires flame
and whiz from decks and rigging, and Chinese lanterns
festoon gear and hulls. An electric arch spans the flag-
ship from stem to stern-post, the night is ablaze, and
here and there through the bright coloring of swinging
lanterns the sharp scintillations of arc and incandescent
lamps punctuate the illuminated page with points of
silvery white. A thousand reflections shimmer in the

water, and from the shores, as the wind serves, the music
of a band drifts over the tide-way. "No use ship-keep-
ing," cries the captain, cheerily. "I must report on board
the flag-ship, but take the boat and strike the beach the
rest of you."

The beams of a search-light make a broad cone about
the gangway as the captains go alongside in their trim gigs.
Here each is received with the etiquette due his uniform,
and after the meeting is called to order the details of
the races are discussed, and the programme of the cruise
is defined and accepted. One can readily see that the
majority of the owners are men of affairs, generally in the
prime of manhood, with a few youngsters here and there,
and others, too, ruddy and strong in the youth of old age.
A few belong to our leisure class — some who cruise the
year round, and others who go in for it, as the phrase is,
during the summer months. Here also are yachtsmen—
not many, but enough to swear by—who have won their
license of the seas by runs across the Atlantic in snow
and ice and killing chill, when the devil was chasing Tom
Coxe up one hatchway and down another, and angry
gales were hurling green seas high above the futtocks of
the fore.

When the meeting is ended, the Commodore enter-
tains the captains until midnight, though some of the
owners leave early to join their guests viewing the illumi-
nation from the shore. In the old days a ball was always
given at the hotel on the night of the rendezvous, but
as men dance so little and under such protest in these
degenerate times, all that has been changed. The verandas and lawns are crowded, and each one of the host
of beautiful women is willing to admit that never before
could there have been such a squadron, such an illumi-
nation, such yachtsmen. After the lights have died out,

DINNER IN THE CABIN

and the chaperons have hoisted a final signal for their fair convoys to slip their moorings and make sail for home, gigs are manned, and with echoing strokes pulled regretfully to the anchorage. The general noises of the squadron have softened into a murmur, and the lights have lessened in cabin and forecastle. The stars, wheeling bright and clear, seem, on these nights, to shine in myriads never known before; and behind the trees a waning moon is dipping. At times the quietness is broken tunefully by mandolin and banjo, and mellowed by distances you hear the refrain of a jolly sea song; and as you pass under the sterns of neighboring boats cheery greetings float to you out of the shadows and from behind the friendly blaze of cigars. The night is too beautiful for sleeping, and you lounge on deck for a while smoking a soothing weed. But after a time, when you have slipped into pyjamas and drained a nightcap to clear the fog and bring good weather, a gentle drowsiness steals upon you, and ere eight bells ring out with silvery notes you are sleeping the dreamless sleep of childhood in a cradle rocked by wind and wave.

V

BRIGHT and early the next morning you are awakened
by the working of the pump, the dashing of water, and the
swishing of brooms overhead; through the air ports steal
the cool, fresh breeze and the light of skies shifting from
gray and silver to blue and gold. Tumbling out, you go
on deck, have a look at wind and weather and at the hands
washing down, and then, hauling on bathing-trunks, fling
yourself overboard in that perfect plunge which makes a
new man of you.

As the start is to be an early one, everybody is astir;
and by the time coffee is finished and you are on deck
again, many of the eager ones are making sail and short-
ening cables, and others have already taken up a commanding position near the starting-point. After a while
the flag-ship and an accompanying boat drop anchor at
either end of an imaginary line, and then, aided by a valorous banging of guns and a brave display of signal flags,
all the yachts cross over the border in due order and precedence, and hot-footed for a competition where only a few
laggards are dragging a penalty allowance behind.

A rare sight this, when the morning is fair and breezy.
Ahead, stretching in great wings and irregularly, now a
cloud of listing, gleaming canvases, here a group struggling as if hand-to-hand in a battle to death, and there,
with open water on both sides, the sloops and cutters rush
for the distant verge. Next, like fairy argosies the great
sloops built to defend the cup dart over the welcoming

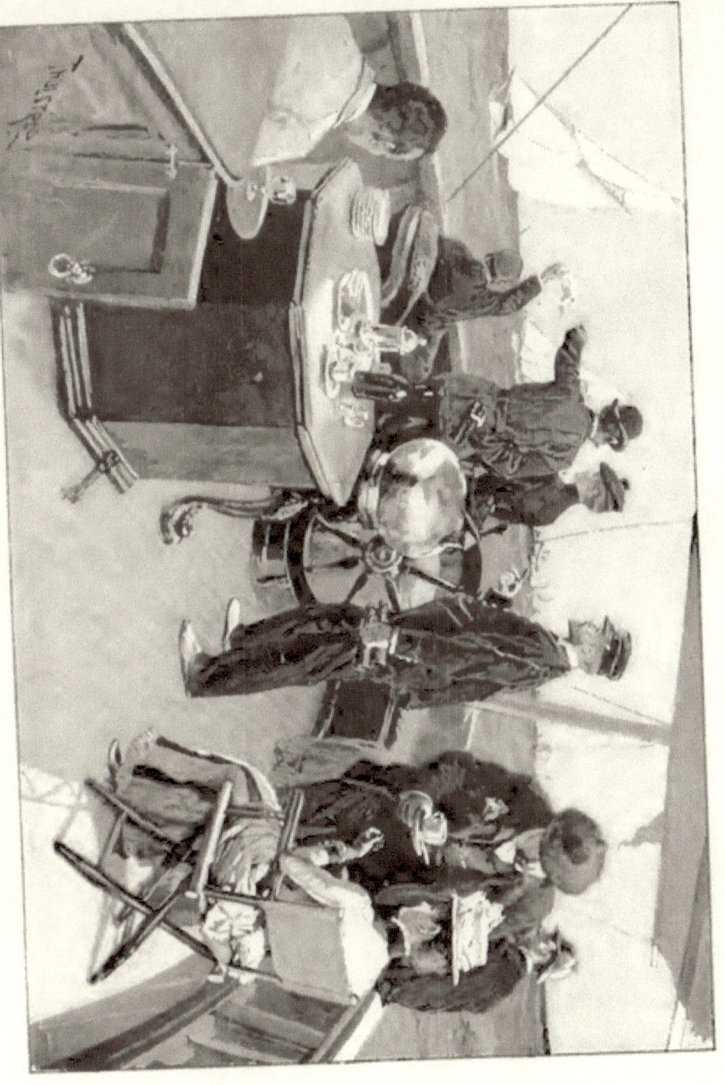

SEEING THE RACE

waves, nothing fairer, nothing truer to eye nor keener to
breeze anywhere in any sea.   Then sweep the stately
schooners, standing up to their work like mitred bishops,
every thread of canvas drawing to tense stretch, the
weather-shrouds taut as harp strings, the wind singing
cheerily through the gear, and the blue water whitening
into wedding blossoms at the bow, and carolling far astern
in a flowery maze of bubbling foam.

The land slips by, the smooth waters of the Sound
merge into Atlantic billows, the skies are blue and steel.
The sun shines warmly, climbs high, and just as you can
see it over the fore-yard of a big steamer, seven bells—
(who will be the poet of that chime?)—ring warningly,
and, with due ceremony, the sacrifice ordained is made,
the libation is poured.

What the origin of this sacred custom, no one knows;
but it is ordered and provided for in the sea law of all nations, and is to be denied under the direst punishment.

The fleetest rush to the van, the dull and careless drop
astern; but no matter, for to clipper ahead and drogher
behind the scene unfolds each moment a beautiful pano-
rama, gives anew that most perfect of pictures, "a ship
sailing upon the water."   When you come on deck from
luncheon, schooners, sloops, and cutters are intermingled;
but if your luck has been good you are at least in the thick
and middle of the fight, and can note the eagerness, the
intelligence, the watchfulness, exercised in the race for
supremacy.   By-and-by gray rocks, seamed with yellow
and green, glint in the sunshine; a light-ship rolls in the
vexed eddies off the reef; the flag-ship sweeps to the fore-
front at her best speed, and soon a gun rings out as the
leader dashes over the line amid the cheers of the hundreds gathered to greet her.

Within a day or two the great cup races are sailed, and,

so that all may see them, the Commodore invites the
yachtsmen not competing, and their guests, to go over the
outside course. When the last event has been decided, a
night reception is given by the flag-ship to the squadron,
and here at its full flood surges the social life of the cruise.
It is everything that such an affair is on shore, multiplied
and intensified by the inherent possibilities of the scene.
And what a picture of pleasure it makes! The brilliant
costumes; the beautiful illuminations; the music; the
view afloat, where hundreds of lanterns are swinging in the
roadstead; and the vistas ashore, where the lights circle
the beaches and climb hillward; the cool breezes, salt with
the savor of thousands of ocean miles bearing them to the
harbor's gates; the plashing of tides; the murmur of
happy voices—well, after all, nothing brings us nearer fairy-
land than a ship, a summer night, a gentle breeze, and the
ripples of distant music.

Somewhat diminished in number, the squadron goes
eastward, stopping at one or two hospitable ports, where
balls ashore and receptions on board break the monotony
of sailing. Then it returns westward, and after the gigs,
dingies, and launches have competed for the traditional
prizes of the clubs, the captains assemble for the last time
on the flag-ship, the vote of thanks to the Commodore is
passed, and, with another fusillade, the Squadron Cruise is
ended.

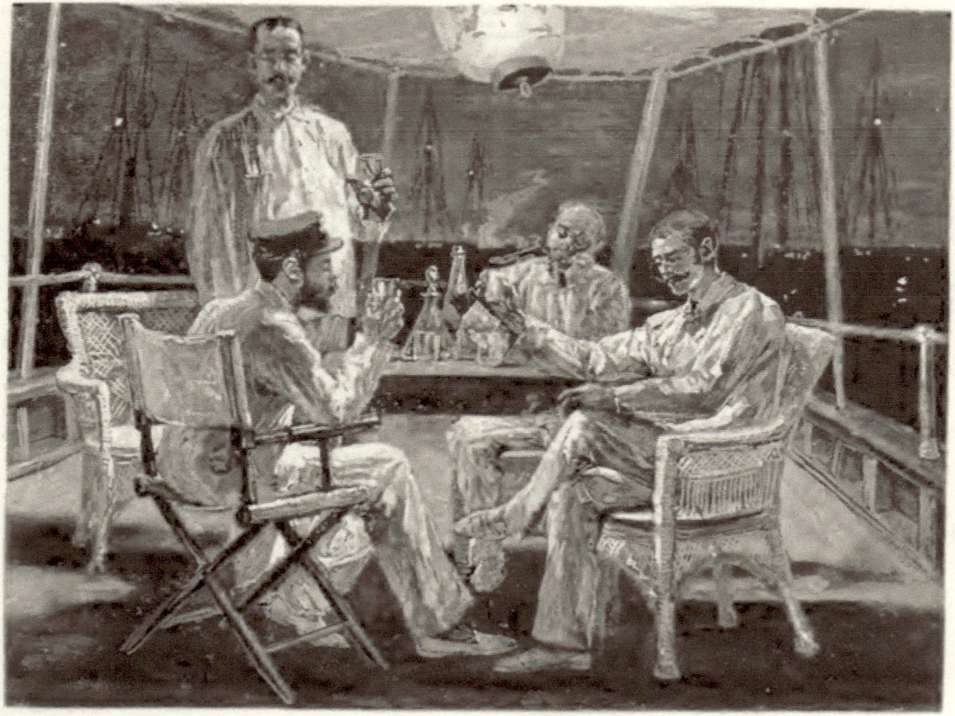

THE NIGHT-CAP

MIDSHIPMEN, OLD AND NEW

MIDSHIPMEN, OLD AND NEW

I

IN a breezy chapter of that delightful volume now almost forgotten, where Kenny Meadows drew and other English Worthies described the Heads of the People, a sailor of the old school laments the decadence of the midshipman. The mast-head, we are told, knew him no more, and his place had been taken by that machine-made product—*the young gentleman*. Fortunately this dismal prophet deserves honor in no country, for is not his growl, more ancient than Benbow's day, the barnacled protest of the Ancient Mariner against the jocund Reefer at the wedding feast, the burden of that litany wherein the elders tell how, since their prime, "the service has gone post-haste to the devil"?

It is of course a far cry from the rattling blades of Nelson's battles to the youngsters who trifle airily with the highest mathematics of our own; but if there be anything in modern progress, the seamen of this year of grace must be, for the demands made upon them, quite as good, let us say, as those who sailed with Jervis and his fleet and humbled the proud Don. No better sea-officers ever lived than those of the last century, none achieved more glory, none left a greater heritage; but they were the results of conditions, the effective though roughly tempered instruments for necessities which to a large

degree have lost their importance. They were survivals
rather of a physical than of an intellectual environment,
so that recalling a training where kicks were many and
ha'pence few, one must be willing to concede the point of
view from which they judged the young officers of their
time. Sent to sea at a tender age, the midshipman of
the last century began his career often in the shock of
battle, always under circumstances rigorous enough to test
the endurance even of the sturdiest man. His school had
no royal tide to learning, and whether he crawled pain-
fully through the hawse-pipes or skipped lightly to the
quarter-deck by the smoother channels of cabins windows,
his education was acquired not in consequence but in
spite of his opportunities. Beyond the art of bowlines
and the science of carronades, knowledge had to be picked
up haphazardly, mainly by unguided observation, somewhat by asking dangerous questions of seniors whose tempers were tried with the asperities of sea-life, and whose
training had convinced them that hard knocks were the
only educational fillips for young sea-boys.

Sometimes a bowing acquaintance was scraped with
the simpler mathematics, through the courtesy of officers
able to devote odd half-hours of rare leisure to such bear-
leading; but this fragmentary instruction was so much
hampered by a hundred interruptions as to make all its
resultant good depend upon individual intelligence and
effort. Occasionally a few midshipmen were enabled to
attend navigation schools previous to joining or while on
leave, and there were instances when the steerage or gun-
room mess was landed on the beach for spasmodic instruction. "During the remainder of the winter," writes Farragut (he was then twelve years old, and attached to the
squadron assembled in 1811 off Newport), "the midshipmen were sent to school to a Mr. Adams." Later,

when he had returned from his cruise on board the *Essex*, he adds, " I was put to school to a queer old individual named Neif, who had no books, but taught orally. The scholars took notes, and were afterward examined on these lectures. In the afternoon it was customary to go for long walks, accompanied by our instructor. On these occasions Mr. Neif would make collections of minerals and plants, and talk to us about mineralogy and botany. We were taught to swim and climb, and were drilled like soldiers." There is a nautical education for you—mineralogy and botany! and yet this pupil of pedagogue Neif became one of the greatest sea-officers the world has known.

On board cruising ships chaplains were enjoined by regulations and tradition to instruct the midshipmen " diligently and faithfully in those sciences appertaining to their department "; but as these reverend gentlemen were not expected to know navigation, seamanship, gunnery, nor foreign languages, the system was hardly broad enough to satisfy an eager craving for professional knowledge. Even at a later date, when school-masters were appointed to the line-of-battle ships, the favored youngsters of these bristling seventy-fours fared no better, for a monthly pay of twenty-five dollars naturally tempted only inferior instructors, who were willing to live with their pupils in steerages or gun-rooms—that is to say, in quarters which at the best were ungirdled by influences apt to lure scholars or teacher into the primrose paths of learning. I know this is heresy to the boyish reader of sea-tales ; for to the lad who has shared the joys, the sweet sorrows, of Jack Easy, Tom Cringle, or the Green Hand, or indeed of any one of the heroes set in the zenith of that galaxy spanning the skies of nautical romance, the steerage or gun-room was ever heaven ; the scene of happiness unalloyed, the home

of darling reefers who own the hearts they won long
years ago, the abode of briny mirth, of tarry jollity, the
stage where, under the dreamiest of lime-lights, Cruik-
shanks's merriest hearts of oak trolled in rousing chorus the sweetest songs Charles Dibdin piped. *O, orbis
pictis!* Oh, deluded youth! The junior officers then
lived, and to a lamentable degree now live, in murky,
dingy, overcrowded, and unwholesome dens, where sunlight entered burglariously and quiet was unknown. To
study within their riotous precincts was as easy as to woo
the coy nightingale in a foundery rattling at white heat,
and to live there required the philosophy of Gil Blas
when the robbers bound hand and foot and threw in their
rate-hole our adventurous nephew of Gil Perez.

Of course these hardships were not provided for nor
emphasized by statutes, and there certainly must have
been laws and privileges for post-captains, and privileges
and laws for midshipmen; but where these last began or
ended, when codified, or to whom lay an appeal, no one
knew. The duties of the youngster, defined neither by
regulation nor tradition, really ebbed and flowed at the
sweet will of the captain, as this was filtered through the
whims of the first lieutenant and skimmed through the
tempers of the watch officers. The midshipmen were at
every one's most selfish beck and call, in everybody's
watch, in nobody's mess, and though punished for two
things only, these were for nothing and for everything.
They were treated as pugilists preparing for a fight, and
were subjected to a rule-of-thumb regimen, which in
hardening the body as often indurated the mind. They
were ordered to work and not to think, and yet at times
the authority, the responsibility given them presupposed
the experience of an intelligent and a highly trained manhood. In his twelfth year Farragut was sent as prize-

SANDY HOOK LIGHT-SHIP BY NIGHT

master of a recaptured merchant ship, with orders to make the best of his way from Guayaquil to Valparaiso—a long stretch this, dead to windward!—and had hardly parted company with the *Essex* before he was called upon to nip a mutiny in a promising bud. And he did it most valorously, pistol in hand. At thirteen he took such a conspicuous part in one of the most gallant sea-fights of our annals that Captain Porter wrote home in his despatches : " Midshipman Farragut deserved the promotion for which he was too young to be recommended." It was after this a grateful country permitted him, at Porter's expense, to attend the school where mineralogy and botany were, and Shakespeare and the musical glasses might have been, a part of his naval schooling.

Unfortunately the training of our first midshipmen did not in peace prepare for war, nor for the conditions peace itself might impose. Their lives were spent at either swing of the pendulum, and as the Jeremiah whose lament introduces this article has declared, their existences were divided into three periods. First, the younker, the Johnny Raw, the first caught, generally an amiable youth with the taste of bread-and-butter still in his mouth, and his sense of perspective dazed at being dubbed *Mister*. At mess his ration was the fattest fag-end of pork and the leanest and most mahogany-grained cubes of salt beef ; under certain guarantees he was allowed to survey the butter and smell the cheese, though as an indemnity his supply of weavily hard biscuit was unlimited. The older messmates showed their paternal care for his health by confiscating his allowance of spirits, and by cheerfully assigning him the privilege — his main duty in port—of going ashore with the captain's steward for milk, and of performing market boat-work generally. At sea, when off watch, the golden hours were passed under the vivifying beams of a

purser's dip, and in an atmosphere redolent of bean soup,
rum, tar, and tobacco, and his leisure was employed in
working out the day's run, or in writing up the log-books
of those bully rooks—his more experienced shipmates. On
watch he called the cooks in the morning, saw the decks
properly swept, tumbled aloft when sails were handled, and
tramped for four hours, off and on, to leeward, or in the
gangways, squeaking out the orders given by the lieutenant in a voice like that of a parrot witlessly maundering
through a cracked reed. If opportunity served he slept
his night-watch stealthily pillowed on a signal flag and
blanketed with a greasy tarpaulin, this bed being spread
under the lee of a quarter-deck gun. At unholy intervals
he was pulled out by the leg from this sea-nest and sent
below to mix and bring up for the deck officer a glass of
grog, strong enough to float a marline-spike. He was most
wantonly badgered and hoaxed everywhere and by every
one, but in the end, before the roses faded in his cheeks
and his crisp locks uncurled in the salted air, he became a
shrewd lad, slow to quarrel, though when driven to it by
excess of persecution ready to fight valorously.

Indeed, he made his way by fighting.

In the second stage, after a year or more of these
civilizing influences, he became wary if not wise, learned
to swear in five languages, by the clock and archaically,
fought for his grog like a fish-wife, and doubled on the
tub whenever the master's mate of the spirit-room for-
bade not in his cups friend nor foe—and this was often.
He knew the names and uses of all the running-gear,
could splice, make a selvagee, and tell how the rigging
went over the mast-head; he learned to muster a watch
when half asleep, and at a pinch could swing a light lead
overhand as far as the lee cathead. After he had grown
a little older, especially if he had seen a fight or two, or

CLEANING BRASSES

been out on a duel, he was respectful to his superiors, attentive to his duties, thoughtful of the blue-jackets, and finical as to the length of his flowing kerchief, to the cockbilling of his shiny hat, to the tautness and bell-mouthing of his trousers, and to the brightness of the anchor-embossed buttons, which shone with the glory of Orion on the dark blueness of his round jacket. He roared no longer as 'twere a nightingale, nor gently as a sucking dove; his voice was larded with holes, though its interrupted hoarseness came not from singing or hal-looing of anthems; and, proud boast of all, his ripening chin knew the barber's shear.

During the third stage, notably, if big in muscle, beamy of shoulder, and two-handed with fists, he became cock of the gunroom walk, Sir Oracle, King Shark of the pilot-fish school. He borrowed more than he loaned, patronized and catered for the mess, took toll of grog from his vassals, drank his stingo to the lees—though this virtuously and discreetly, for, like Master Slender in the play, he caroused only with the sober-minded and in exemplary society. There was observance in his eye, activity in his heels, humility in the hinges of his knees. From his seniors he took everything in good part; dinner with the captain joyously; reproof from watch officers humbly; lunars with the master assiduously; and conceit out of his juniors boastfully. "Though he knoweth," concludes the nautical entomologist who has pinned this extinct specimen in his cabinet, "that he be now in the chrysalis state, he anticipateth with an overstrained faith the time when he will burst forth, the butterfly lieutenant with the golden wing on his right shoulder, and he prideth himself accordingly. Thus there be three states of this officer, yet is he one and indivisibly a midshipman."

5

II

LIVING amid such influences and hardships, it is not easy to understand how the officers who entered the service at the end of the last century and the beginning of this learned so admirably the duties they had subsequently to perform as commanders of ships and squadrons. Treated by the government with shameful neglect, and denied adequate training, they earned through native wit and sheer energy the respect of foreign officers more happily nurtured. Intrusted with the fortunes of their own country, and consecrated to the illustration of freedom's universal truths, they commanded the admiration and respect of the most civilized nations by personal qualities and by professional accomplishments which, though self-acquired, luckily included an intimate knowledge of international law. By bravery in battle, skill in naval tactics, modesty in victory, intrepidity in defeat, wisdom in council, tact in diplomacy, and, best of all, courage in asserting the higher obligations of morals and of natural laws, they made piracy in the Barbary States and the denial of the seaman's rights upon the high seas equally, and for all time, odious.

Called by their duties to seas of activity where the just proportions and relativities of all countries could be measured, they were among the first to prophesy the possibilities of the new republic; their wider horizons dissipated the mists of prejudice, and in the pure white light they recognized this nation's geographical importance, and foretold its coming influence as the World's Great Middle Kingdom. They knew the perils that would beset it, they emphasized its necessities of offence and defence, and, conscious of the cruel difficulties which had encumbered their own careers, they begged Congress to make the navy, by a *personnel* properly selected and trained, equal to any demands. In season and out, through good fortune and ill, they persisted in this fight. It was a long, a wearisome struggle for recognition and justice, but these old officers and their successors never faltered, and in the end succeeded so well that the Naval Academy, organized in 1845 by George Bancroft, then Secretary of the Navy, is their monument and witness.

Honor to both—to the officers who fought fifty years for its establishment, and to the historian who realized their ambition.

III

THE students of this national college are called officially "naval cadets on probation," the traditional title of midshipman having been changed first to cadet midshipman, and subsequently—so the engineer pupils might be included—to that now employed. Their number is limited by law to one cadet for each Congressional district, one for each territory, and to eleven others—ten at large and one from the District of Columbia — appointed by the President. As the age of admission now falls between the limits of fifteen and twenty, and the course extends six years, it follows, unfortunately, that in certain districts appointments may not be open more than once in that period, thus making one-third of its boys unavailable by reason of age. The remedy proposed for this is only one of fifty good reasons why the course should be reduced from six to four years, and the age of admission limited to not less than fifteen nor more than seventeen.

To pass, the candidate must be physically sound and of robust constitution, have a sufficiently thorough knowledge of arithmetic, algebra, geography, English grammar, United States history, reading, writing, and spelling, and, when appointed, be ready to take an oath to serve for eight years, including the probationary period. When a vacancy is likely to occur in any district, the Secretary of the Navy must notify its Congressional Representative as soon as possible after the 5th of March, and if by the 1st of the following July no action has been taken,

EIGHT BELLS—COLORS

the privilege lapses, and the Secretary is empowered to make the nomination. As this system permits the choice of a candidate and his alternate to be deferred until the May examination is really over, or, as in the majority of cases, until the academic year is about to open, it would seem to be better if the candidate and alternate were named at least one year previous to the May examination. This would enable the applicant to pursue a special course, well fitted as a direct preparation for his professional studies, and when he passed to go at once upon a cruise, which would teach him definitely his aptitude for life at sea. On the other hand, should the principal fail, the alternate would stand ready to face the same ordeal.

This standard of admission, confessedly low, is based upon the theory that the possibilities of the academy must be open so freely to boys of every condition as to make it —like the military school at West Point—an essentially democratic government school. Practically this very just theory impairs the efficiency of the academy, as it pins the qualifications at a point which rigorously forbids the energies of the teacher and of the average scholar being directed immediately to the branches of education connected with the naval profession. It may as well be stated, to disarm sentimental criticism, that no extravagant standard of admission is desired by the advocates of this change; all they ask for is that thorough preliminary training which every public and district school should, but to a startling degree does not, give. I know this is a delicate question to approach, but one may risk it if he is sure the fact will be kept in evidence that the academy was established, not to furnish an education to certain favored persons, but to train officers equally selected from the whole country for its service afloat. If these interests are alone to be considered,

surely, here as everywhere, the methods and materials best
suited should be adopted, and this means, at the very least,
that where the tuition of the best common schools should
end, that of the academy ought to begin. The institution
belongs to the people, and must be and is open to every
district in this country, but it does seem as if those States
and Territories which are the first to cry out against a superior standard ought to improve their own educational
methods rather than seek to lower those of the nation.
Whatever people may say, the academy is not a rich man's
school, and it is hardly a valid objection to insist that with
a higher standard the sons of the poor will be excluded,
because the establishment of almost any test would be,
somewhere, a discrimination in this sense. So far as the
methods of making nominations go, there are many pertinent inquiries which might be considered, notably that re-
lating to the value of competitive examinations. Much can
be advanced for and against this theory, but its discussion
may be dismissed here with the statement that experience
has so far proved its superiority. At the military academy
this is notably the case, for of 502 appointments secured
by competition, 306—sixty-one per cent.—were graduated,
as opposed to 280—or forty-four per cent.—of direct nominations.

THE LIFE-BOAT DRILL

IV

ENTRANCE examinations are held in May and September, and should the candidate be nominated in time to attend the first, he sees the academy under its most favorable light. At this season the Annapolis spring is ripe with the promises of early summer in the North. Skies are bright, breezes are brisk, and the shining water and the air, laden with the perfume of growing grasses and of bourgeoning buds, fill the drowsy old colonial capital with the sweet suggestions of the earth's new birth. Bayward, miles away, the woodlands of Kent Island lift a barrier of green to the tideways of the Chesapeake, and, in days when light and wind are favorable, the shadowy Eastern Shore is silhouetted on the sky, and the spires of Cambridge glint spectrally in the silvery mirage. Within the academy walls trees and shrubbery are dowered with leaf and blossom, and shoreward, sometimes in terraces, often with inclines so gentle as hardly to be traced, the trim lawns steal to the river's banks. Streets silvered with the sun-filtered tracery of leaves, and rambling roadways, reveal beneath the arching branches new vistas at every turn. Near the lower gate the library—for more than a hundred years the residence of Maryland's colonial and state Governors —is so happily situated as to merit the praise which, even as far back as 1769, confessed that "but few mansions in the most rich and cultivated parts of England are adorned with such splendid and romantic scenery." Stretching on either side, between the marine barracks at the southeast

and the cadets' new quarters at the northwest, are the
chapel, officers' quarters, and hospital. Nearer the riverfront the armory and laboratory flank the steam-engineering building, and farther southward the observatory, mu-
seum, seamanship and recitation halls join the old cadet
quarters, now used principally as offices and as apartments
for the bachelor instructors. At right angles to these, and
almost in line with the library, the quaint, high-dormered
houses, dating from army days, look with disparaging eyes
upon the spick-and-span freshness of the superintendent's
house, and thank the fates which have given them a gen-
tility, a little faded, a little shabby, it may be, but real,
and still redolent of the good old times. Where the Sev-
ern meets an inlet from Chesapeake Bay, Windmill Point
breasts with easy curve the shallow water and carries, behind the gun park at its edge, the old circular fort, now a
gymnasium, but once a warlike redoubt bristling with a
terrific defiance of pop-guns for the foe that never came.
War-ships, allotted for purposes of instruction, swing at
their anchorages in the river, and flotillas of steam-
launches and sailing cutters cluster about a long wharf
that reaches deep water and holds in safe moorings the
practice-ships and the school-ship *Santee*. A quiet, peaceful landscape fitly frames all this, for these school-days
prelude lives that will be filled with many a struggle in
stormy seas to be.

Should it be band hour or recreation-time, the lawns
and pathways are thronged with visitors, among them
mothers, sisters, and sweethearts, who saunter with their
young heroes in navy blue under the maples embowering
Love Lane, or along the pleasant road, wandering maze-
like by the granite shaft that tells how Herndon died. If
the candidate is bitten by the tarantula of anticipatory
delight, he riots in the dissipations of drills looked at,

when he ought to be "boning" for the examination near
at hand; and his eyes kindle and his cheeks glisten as he
sees the artillery battalion rushing in quick time, in column
of platoons, down the campus and into the lower grounds.
Drag-ropes are tense, wheels are rattling, red-cheeked
cadets scamper over the soft ground with springy feet,
and there, where the bay view opens, a shrill command
rings out, "Fire to the front! Right front into line! In
battery! Ma-a-a-a-rch!" and in an instant the stage is
transformed at a bugle-call. Where were guided ranks
and rigidly dressed pieces is now the gleam of guns dart-
ing forward and sideways at every angle; a jumble of
tossing arms, of nimble legs, of white-gaitered feet, of flut-
tering guidons, and of waving banners. With sharp distinctness voices repeat the orders and mingle with the
spinning of spoke-hidden wheels, the jangle and jar of
quickly swung trail-pieces, and the clattering of ammuni-
tion-boxes; and then a loud "bang" awakens the echoes,
rumbling hillward. Through the enshrouding smoke
dimly limned figures are seen loading and firing, and
other forms, spectrally outlined in the powder fog, dash
backward and forward between the guns and their quarter-
gunner at the rear. At last the bugle rings with clarion
call, "Cease firing!" and after the inevitably late piece
has had its deferred but obstinately last word, the fight
is ended, the day is gallantly won.

V

WHEN the candidate has passed the mental and physical examinations, he reports to the superintendent, takes
the oath of allegiance, and deposits twenty dollars for his
books, and such an additional sum as may be required for
the official outfit. This amount is specified annually, but
this represents everything, and from it there is always de-
ducted the value of such clothing brought from home as
need not be of standard pattern. One month after admission he is credited with his actual travelling expenses to
the academy, though this must be refunded if he resigns
voluntarily within a year. His annual pay is about $610
—$500 pay proper, and one daily ration valued at thirty
cents. This begins at appointment, but while he acknowl-
edges its receipt and expenditure, his control over it is
purely nominal. He pays for books, clothing, mess, laundry, barber — indeed, for everything; and all these expenses, after being certified by him and approved by the
superintendent, are paid and charged monthly to his account. Every year sixty dollars are reserved from his
pay for a graduation outfit, and according to his conduct
he receives a monthly reward of pocket-money, usually
so microscopic as to keep him in the traditionally im-
pecunious condition that everywhere is the hall and mint
mark of a midshipman. Luckily, all his stores are supplied at first cost, and that the purchasing power of his
money is high may perhaps be illustrated by the fact that
in his annual dentistry bills—and his teeth are most rig-

ARTILLERY BATTALION

orously and capably cared for — only the actual cost of
the gold is charged.

When his immediate material necessities are settled, he
is assigned by the commandant of cadets to his duties in
the preliminary routine, is allowed to sport a uniform cap,
and ordered to report on board the *Santee*. Unless he is a
very good boy indeed, this is apt not to be his only acquaintance with the school-ship. Usually he becomes very
nautical at once, and the earliest of his ambitions is to go
aloft, "to mount," as the shore poet has chastely put it,
"the dizzy tops"; but the gun or berth deck claims him
as its own, and his first maritime achievement—slinging
the hammock which will be his bed for the next two
months or more—teaches him that in ways marine his
fingers are all thumbs. He takes a keen delight in ordering his outfit and in stowing his locker with a kit that
grows wondrously, and he is somewhat startled, like his
forebears, with the courtesy which immediately splices
Mister to his name.

The earliest experiences of the cadet are not in harmony
with his new dignity ; he is not altogether happy, for while
he suffers from no direct hazing, and undergoes no such
"running" as my contemporaries endured, still the thinly
disguised contumely, the silent though stinging scorn of
the fourth-class men, are hard to bear. His awkwardness
at formations are not soothed with fraternal sympathy—
except he be a Kentuckian, for the cadets from that State
are traditionally clannish, and nearly always *claim* kinship.
His *gaucheries* at the mess-table by the door—plebe's paradise, as it is called—are sins for which he does long pen-
ances, and whenever occasion serves his milk is boldly
confiscated, and he is made to feel that, after all is said
and done, his salvation is yet to be worked out by parlous
essay. He drills twice a day, is taught the school of the

soldier, and in artillery the school of section, and has a
daily swimming-lesson.   His envy of the senior classes
grows hourly, and his admiration and respect for the first-
class men are memories rarely forgotten, even after he has
attained their place, and gone out into the service which
in time levels so many academic distinctions.   Then comes
to him, of course, as to all boys at any school, moments
of depression and homesickness, and he wonders at the
delusions which made him take the people's shilling; he
loathes Marryat, forswears Cooper, denies Michael Scott,
derides Cupples, and when the night comes, and he tosses
feverishly in his hammock—a stranger in a strange land—
the poor lad thinks lovingly of his father's home.   Finally
the academic year closes, his two or more weeks of *Santee*
life are ended, and with beating heart and happy anticipa-
tion he joins the practice-ship, and on a bright June morning sees the senior cadets tumble aloft, watches the top-
sails mast-headed, and discovers that, at last, he is fairly
away for his first shivering cruise.   Before this is ended
he has learned a great deal of marline-spike seamanship,
and has decided definitely as to his fitness for the profession.

For a week or two he has drills, but no studies, and his
days are set in ways which, after all, are but a pleasant
overture before the prompter's bell lifts the curtain from
a stage where, major or minor though his part be, earnest
labor is expected.   These are rare days, too, in anticipa-
tion, and so filled with high resolves, let us hope, that the
end of September, when the leave men return, is welcomed
gladly.

The next day studies begin.

VI

THE academic year is divided into two terms, the first ending on the Saturday nearest January 30th, the second upon the last day of May, and during these eight months cadet life follows a routine which is carefully adjusted to the results demanded. It is a season of honest labor, of mental progress, of physical growth, and the system, rich in brain and brawn development for the studious, is relentless only for the idle and careless. Though the course exacts unremittent effort, it is not a bloodless mechanism imposing upon boys the burden men only should bear, nor is it a race where the pace is set for genius alone. Whatever ignorance or prejudice may assert, the records of many years prove that of 855 appointments, 467, or nearly fifty-five per cent., were graduated, and that sixty-six per cent. of the candidates who entered between fourteen and fifteen years of age completed the four years' course, as compared with fifty-two per cent. of those admitted between the ages of seventeen and eighteen. Above all things, the contest is a fair one, and as the political or social influences controlling appointments no longer serve, success is handmaiden only to an individual merit that is denied assistance from without or favor from within. The environment supposes the student to be a grateful beneficiary of a government which has selected him for its present care, future honors, and life-long consideration, and which expects that earnest study will be allied to the obedience and subordination demanded in a naval career.

The new cadet is assigned to the fourth or lowest class, and becomes a unit in an organization assimilating, as far as may be, with that of a ship of war. He is assigned to one of sixteen crews grouped in four divisions, each of which is made up of equal proportions of the different classes. His immediate superiors are two cadet petty officers, chosen from the senior classes, and known as First and Second Captains. Four crews form a division, commanded by a Cadet Lieutenant, and officered with a Cadet Junior-Lieutenant and Cadet Ensign, all first-class men. These four divisions make a battalion, having for its chief a Cadet Lieutenant Commander, and for its Adjutant an additional Cadet Lieutenant. Special privileges are enjoyed by the student officers, and orders coming through them are official and must be obeyed. At drills and practical exercises each crew mans a great gun, a howitzer section, or a boat, and each division forms a howitzer battery, a gun division, an infantry company, or a boat squadron. The various details demanded of a cadet are apt, in the beginning, to confuse a mind already disturbed by new impressions and influences, but experience soon forges a master-key that, before long, opens easily the doors of many mysteries. Among other surprises, infantry drill enters so much into his daily life that he who has dreamed of swelling sails and tugging sheets and billows rolling free, finds the first step in his career to be the goose-step, and that his days and nights are infested with the cares of formations, and filled with bugle-calls which, as they blow him out of bed, sound but faintly as horns of elf-land winding clear. Ah! those first reveilles, those awful reveilles are ever rude awakenings, and is it a wonder the homesick, half-aroused boy discovers life to be lonesome enough when the gray daylight makes his windows in the four-story back slowly grow a glimmering square? He lives

in the New Quarters, and an uglier residence devoted to
equal interests is not to be found the world over.

With the best intentions, it must be confessed that the
academy is not happy in its buildings. Its architects did
not keep pace with the school's progress in other directions, nor indeed profit by the examples of sincere art the
old colonial town offers at their hearth-stones. There is a
trim rigidity of limb about most of the structures which
gives one as a first and most lasting impression the convic-
tion that these, like the old sailing sloops of war, were surely built by the mile, and cut off in lengths to suit a fluct-
uating appropriation. A few of the older houses—such,
I mean, as have not had their gifts improved away—are
quaintly dignified, and one or two of the newer buildings
have luckily escaped the rigors of Gunter's scale and dead
reckoning; but the New Quarters are *anathema mara-
natha*. They are hard-faced and gradgrindy; their want of
grace is accentuated by their site, and their ugliness is
emphasized by the curves and lines of the monument sulk-
ing in their shadow. Were it not for a pseudo-mauresque,
a sort of far-away-Moses piazza on the main building,
this misplaced watch factory might be supposed to have
stepped out between two days from the first book of
Chauvenet's geometry. But apart from all considerations
of beauty and fitness, the quarters are badly built, poorly
ventilated, and so inadequate that their overcrowded limits
are encroached upon by kitchens, store-rooms, and a mess-
hall, which, from sanitary reasons, ought to be in a separate building.

Two cadets are quartered in a room, and as discipline,
like charity, begins at home, here at the very threshold,
the hardening processes commence. The surroundings
are rigorously simple, as needs must be in a school organized upon the theory that the appointments which ex-

tinguish distinctions of wealth forbid its manifestations. Everything within the room conforms to a standard pattern, and as the display of unauthorized articles is a misdemeanor, this regulation is rarely violated. The room is always in charge of a cadet, and during this weekly tour of duty, which begins at reveille on Sunday morning, he is responsible for its cleanliness, for the government property, and for any violations of interior discipline. He must sweep and arrange it carefully each morning for inspection, and in a bill of particulars as long as the main-to-bowline he is directed what the outfit must be, how it must be arranged, and what care must be taken of it. He has an iron bedstead, a wooden chair, a wash-stand, a looking-glass, a rug, and a wardrobe; the table he shares with his room-mate. No curtains, maps, nor pictures may be hung, nails may not be driven into walls or wood-work, the books in actual use alone may be in evidence, and the gas may be lighted only when authorized. During study hours a cadet may not visit another room, nor be absent from his own unnecessarily; and as he is not allowed to sit up after taps, prepare food, or give the slightest entertainment in his quarters, those diluted Walpurgis-night festivals so dear to the undergraduate marrow, so deadly to the matriculating digestion, are unhonored and unsung. "Though a fiddle," says the sea-proverb, "is as good as ten men on a tackle, and the best muscle not half so strong as a cheery chantey," yet is the cadet forbidden to practise upon any musical instrument during study hours, or at any time on Sunday, even if his psalmody seeks to lift itself in praise "with trumpets, also shawms."

Loud talking, boisterous conduct, and skylarking mean demerits innumerable, and the *Santee's* deepest deeps yawn for the hardened sinner who, like Powhatan in the play, is caught blowing away his cares with a dudeen,

MAN OVERBOARD

raising the limit on a bobtail flush, or—*horresco referens*—looking upon the Annapolis wine when it is red in the cup. Of course many of the hard-and-fast regulations are broken, but rarely in serious matters, because the system is one of severe discipline for misdemeanors and of liberal privileges for good conduct. Hence in the lowest, most material sense, it does not pay to be in trouble, for this denies a student the cakes and ale, and ginger hot i' the mouth too, of academy life. Then there are traditions stronger than any fear of punishment, which are apt to keep the youngster straight in the course he ought to steer; for, with Hotspur, he is taught to think, "I am not covetous of gold, but if it be a sin to covet honor, I am the most offending soul alive." In many ways the cadet can never escape an unobtrusive but unwearied surveillance, and in others his liberty of action is untrammelled, simply because he is on his honor not to violate a confidence of which, with his crew, class, or corps, he is a co-trustee.

The duty of inspection and the care of discipline are delegated to the commandant of cadets, and to assistants, who are always graduates. The detail is taken in rotation, and continues for twenty-four hours, during which period the officer in charge is always a very busy and often a much-bothered personage. He inspects the battalion at roll-call, attends formations, is present at mess, visits the quarters at regular, and, what is harrowing to the cadet soul, at irregular hours, and, above all, sees that all violations of discipline are checked and reported. Two first-class men, assigned each morning, assist him in these duties, and so, day in and day out, the wheels of discipline roll in well-oiled grooves, and the life of the school runs from start to finish briskly, happily, earnestly, with hands down, head free, and curb that rarely frets.

6

VII

SUMMER and winter reveille arouses the cadet at six
o'clock; three-quarters of an hour later he attends morning roll-call, and marches to breakfast. The purchase and
service of mess supplies, the mess outfit, and the bill of
fare are duties intrusted to a naval paymaster. Every
cadet pays a mess entrance fee, but this is charged against
his account, and is refunded when he leaves the academy.
His monthly assessment for mess bill and laundry averages
about $22; but if for any reason he is absent on leave for
a week or longer, he receives credit for this absence on his
mess account. The officer in charge presides at meals, has
charge of the police of the mess-hall, and inspects it and
the servants daily. The food is well cooked, neatly served,
and furnished with the liberality and the variety demanded by growing youths whose bodies and minds are at a
healthy strain. The bill of fare is not moulded months
ahead in cast-iron schedules, but is arranged from day
to day, so that appetites may be sharpened by the
gifts which one of the best markets in the world—Baltimore—offers at the very door of the school. Breakfast
lasts thirty minutes, and the chaplain then reads morning
prayers. During the half-hour recreation which follows,
" sick call " is sounded, and cadets who are ill, or who think
they are incapacitated for full routine of studies and drills,
report to the surgeon. This officer prepares a list of those
excused from drills, and another of those whose ailments
are serious enough to forbid all work. Should these latter

cases require constant supervision, they are sent to the Sick Quarters.

For the purpose of study and recreation the day is divided into three periods of two hours each, the first period commencing at 7.55 and ending at 10.10 A.M.; the second extending from 10.20 A.M. to 12.35 P.M.; and the third from 1.50 to 3.55 P.M. Each cadet, as a rule, attends three recitations daily, and as the routine is regulated so that he is seldom obliged to recite more than once in the same period, he has an hour of study previous to each lesson, in addition to the two hours which he is expected to employ at night in general preparation. The course of instruction is grouped under the special departments of (1) Seamanship, Naval Construction, and Naval Tactics; (2) Ordnance and Gunnery; (3) Astronomy, Navigation, and Surveying; (4) Steam-engineering; (5) Mechanics and Applied Mathematics; (6) Physics and Chemistry; (7) Mathematics; (8) English Studies, History, and Law; (9) Modern Languages; (10) Mechanical Drawing; and (11) Physiology and Hygiene. This last includes "instruction in the nature of alcoholic drinks and narcotics, with special reference to their effects upon the human system."

The faculty, known here as the Academy Board, consists of the Superintendent, the Commandant of Cadets, and the eleven heads of departments. These are naval officers, and mainly graduates of the academy. The direct supervision of the institution is given by law to the Secretary of the Navy, but its government is assigned to a superintendent, who must be a line officer, not below the grade of commander (lieutenant-colonel in relative army rank). The *personnel* and *matériel* are under his command, and he can appoint or remove all employés whose tenures do not come within the special provisions of law or regulations. The enforcement of interior discipline and

the direction of drills and tactical instruction are intrusted
to the Commandant of Cadets, who must also be a line
officer not below the grade of commander.   In all studies
the instruction is supervised by the heads of departments,
each one distributing its work among the assistants assigned to his special branch.   Without going into more
burdensome details than are unavoidable, it may be said
that the academic course extends over four years, and is
divided as follows: Fourth class, Algebra, Geometry, English History, Rhetoric, and French; third class, Trigonom-
etry, Descriptive Geometry, Analytic Geometry, English
History, the Constitution, Elementary Physics, Chemistry,
French, and Mechanical Drawing; second class, Marine
Engines and Boilers, Sound, Light, and Heat, Electricity,
Magnetism, Calculus, Mechanics, and International Law;
and first class, Seamanship, Naval Tactics, Ordnance, Gunnery, Astronomy, Navigation, Surveying, and Physiology
and Hygiene.   It will be seen from this that the first three
years are devoted mainly to a general education, and that
in the last year the course is technically adapted to the
naval service, more particularly to the duties of line officers.   At the close of the academic term of four years
the cadets are distributed among the cruising vessels where
this professional tendency is supposed to be continued,
though, it must be confessed, this is more or less perfunctory, except in practical matters.   Two years after graduation the cadets are gathered from all over the world, subjected to a final examination, and assigned such relative
positions among themselves, in the grade of ensign, as
their examination rank and cruise reports may determine.

With much that is good in this system goes much that
is evil, and radical changes should be made in it.   Nowhere are the demands for these changes more earnestly
and intelligently advocated than at the Academy, and if

GOING ALOFT

Congress would consider the suggestions made by the
Superintendent, and indorsed by the Secretary, certain
measures of relief would be certain to follow. First of all,
the course should be reduced to four years, and at its
conclusion the selections for the various corps should be
made, and the surplus graduates be honorably discharged.
There are, in an educational sense, no arguments in favor
of the two years' course afloat, and the examination to be
passed at its end must, from the conditions imposed upon
the cadets by ship life, be similar in nature to that already
passed at the end of the four years' course. Upon going
afloat, at the end of the academic term, the varying conditions of ship, station, and surroundings must be of such
undue advantage to some, and of such great disadvantage
to others, that should it be considered advisable to retain
the six years' course, the entire class ought, in all fairness,
to be placed on board the same ship and be subjected to
the same systematic training and discipline. There can be
no question of the unnecessary expense and hardship of
subjecting those who are reasonably sure, from their academic standing, to be surplus graduates to an additional
course afloat which tends to unfit them for civil pursuits;
and, on the other hand, it is only right that a naval cadet
should, at graduation, be given, as at West Point, a commission which will remove him as early as possible from
the probationary state.

Leaving out all question as to the modernity and ade-
quacy of the curriculum, what seems most to be needed are
provisions that the period of admission should be limited
to ages between fifteen and seventeen, inclusive; that in
order to give opportunities for proper preparation, the appointments should be made one year in advance; that entrance should be authorized only in May, and not, as at
present, in May and September; that the length of the

course should be four years, and that, at its expiration, graduates entering the service should be commissioned in the lower grade of the line and of the engineer and marine corps, and those not entering should be given an honorable discharge.

Whatever may be said of the defects of the system, no faults may be found with its conduct, for its fine results have been due largely to the loyalty and ability of those intrusted with its control.   There are given to every detail an economy of labor and a fruition of energy which forbid the vain conservatism that sacrifices results to methods, and looks rather to the perfection of the machinery than to the work expected of the machine.

VIII

RECITATIONS are heard by sections, which usually include from five to ten students, so that all instruction is largely individual and direct. While this imposes a great burden upon the teachers, still it is borne with a patience that entitles these gentlemen to the gratitude of the country. Besides these mental benefits, a personal direction is kept over the student's physical setting up—to his manner of entering and leaving the room, to his bearing at the black-board, to his attitude while at rest. The value of a recitation is estimated by a scale of marks ranging from 4 as a maximum to zero, all intermediate numerical qualities representing such other relations that 2.5 is a minimum of proficiency, and all marks below this are unsatisfactory. ʹEvery study day, except Saturday, there is a drill or exercise which begins at 4.05 P.M., and may continue until 5.30 P.M. Though this instruction is distributed under forty heads, it may be grouped, for illustration, under the general branches of Seamanship, Gunnery, Infantry Drill, Naval Tactics, Small Arms, Signalling, Navigation, Surveying, Steam and Practical Electricity, Dancing, and Physical Exercise. Drills are strictly progressive, and are held usually by divisions, though at intervals the corps is assembled for general instruction. The fourth class is taught Seamanship—mainly rigging-loft work —Great-Gun Exercise, Infantry Tactics, Field Artillery, Rowing, Swimming, and Dancing. The next year the three last are omitted, and Fencing and Target Practice

with muskets and pistols are added.   In the second class
the target practice is extended to Great Guns and Ma-
chine-pieces, and there is a capital practical course in
Steam Machinery and Signalling.   In the first-class year
Steam Tactics, Monitor Exercise, Great-Gun Target Practice, Torpedoes, Navigation, Surveying, Practical Electricity, and Boxing complete the course.   Gunnery, Seamanship, and Steam Exercises take place at anchor and under way, so that before the four years are ended each
cadet has received individual instruction in the details of
these sciences, from the manual labor of a landsman, coal-
heaver, and powderman, up to the command of the ship
and battery, and to the charge of the machinery under
way.   After the daily drill there is a recreation period until evening roll-call at 6.30.   This is followed by supper
and another recreation period which ends at 7.30.   Studies continue until 9.30, and then with gun-fire and tattoo
the day's work is over.   For a happy half-hour books and
drills and all the petty cares and failures of the hour are
forgotten; the grim building is merry with boyish voices;
the tinkle of guitars, the resonant twang of banjos, and
the chorus of old-day songs are heard.   But body and
mind are tired, and by-and-by lights disappear, voices
grow lower, the bugles sound taps, and, as if by magic,
the quarters slip into darkness, and the cadet's long day
is done.

Such is the brief and colorless record of daily life at the
academy.   Summed up, it gives a student eight hours for
sleep, five and a half for studies, three for recitations, two
for drills and formations, one and a half for mess, and four
for recreation, though during this play-time official interruptions often make his leisure less than one-sixth of the
day.   Saturday is a half-holiday, and studies and recitations end at 10.10 A.M., and drills at 12.30 P.M.   After

Sunday inspection or muster, church service is held. This is non-sectarian, and attendance is obligatory, except with cadets who have, at the written request of their parents or guardians, received permission to attend the Annapolis churches of their home faiths. These church parties march to and from town in charge of a senior cadet, who is expected to maintain order and report violations of discipline.

Written examinations take place monthly, and the academic standing for that period is determined by adding the mean of a cadet's weekly average (multiplied by two) to the examination marks, and then dividing the sum by three. A statement of this standing, together with the number of demerits received and the relative class rank attained, is bulletined for the information of the corps, and forwarded monthly to the cadet's parents and to the Secretary of the Navy. Sometimes different formulæ for determining averages are employed, but in every case the essential principle is the same. The semi-annual and annual examinations are written, and every paper submitted is examined and marked separately by two instructors, and all oral examinations must be conducted in the presence of the head of the department.

Objection is sometimes made that the standard of scholarship is so artificial or so arbitrary—mainly in the preponderance given to mathematical attainments—as to drive out of the service many cadets who otherwise would make capital officers. But is this true? I believe not, for it is claimed years of experience prove that those who have the best standing in the pure or applied mathematics show also higher capacity and superior industry in the other branches. The board of visitors of 1884 made a special investigation of this subject, and its conclusions are worth quoting. "A numerical standard," it reports, "is purely nominal, and at best only approximate. The chief

practical question is as to its administration and applica-
tion. A careful inspection has surprised the board that
the standards of this school are interpreted and applied
with the utmost intelligence and liberality. Nothing
more is required than is fairly necessary to the efficiency
of the public service. Every reasonable indulgence is allowed, every proper opportunity is offered to make good
deficiencies within reasonable limits, and every possible
encouragement is given to the cadet from the beginning
to the end of the course. The records are kept with the
utmost fulness, precision, and impartiality, and the standards of scholarship, as well as of merit and demerit in
conduct grades, are applied with discretion and leniency.
Every student gets the fullest credit for attainment and
for conduct, and it is difficult to see what better system
could be devised or how any system could be better administered."

So the busy year runs away, but not unhappily, for
though these details may seem as joy-productive as the
Homeric enumeration of the ships, still cadet life is not all
work and no play, and our nautical Jack is far from being
a dull boy. He has his breathing-spaces, his privileges,
his amusements. On Saturday afternoons leave is granted
—its frequency depending upon the student's standing
and conduct; the first grade going weekly, the next every
fortnight, and the immortals of the last division but once
a month. This liberty begins at dinner formation, and
continues for the first class until gun-fire at 9.30 P.M., and
for the others until evening roll-call. In addition to these
general privileges, a first or second class man in the highest conduct grade has leave on Sunday afternoons, and,
where especially good behavior and standing warrant the
privilege, permission is given to visit Baltimore or Wash-
ington. Though this seems rather hard on the pent-up

FURLING THE TOP-SAIL

third grade, still these careless young gentlemen do not suffer as much as might be imagined, for, at the best, Annapolis is a dull town, and nearly all amusements are found within the academy walls. Naturally these take the form of athletic exercises and competitions. There are class clubs of all kinds, and of course an academy crew, nine, and eleven for stirring holiday matches with the athletes of Johns Hopkins, Princeton, Georgetown, or St. John's, and with their brother cadets at West Point, until for some occult reason this was forbidden. The contests are managed by an association, and are financially supported by a fixed monthly contribution, and by a tax which is ingeniously raised through the proposition that "all cadets who do not wish to contribute towards a new boat [for example] will please leave their names with the officer of the day." Need it be added that public spirit rises superior to the twenty-five or fifty cents expected, and that the officer of the day's aged and mouldy list has been in all these years a *tabula rasa?* During recreation hour the tennis-courts, pistol-gallery, and bowling-alley may be used, and on Saturdays the trim steam-launches and graceful sailing cutters are at the disposition of those who, like Pepys, "will take by boat a holiday in merry company."

Hops are given in the gymnasium Saturday nights after Thanksgiving, and twice a year two large balls make joyous the hearts of many maidens whose dreams for weeks previous have revolved in a circle, the centre of which is the band-stand in the armory, where these entertainments take place. During the winter the officers have private theatricals, to which the cadets are invited, and an annual tournament enables the first-class men to exhibit their strength and grace as swordsmen, club-swingers, boxers, and ground and lofty tumblers. Every form of legitimate sport, except that much-missed annual football match with West Point, is encouraged by the superintendent, and so when the annual examination comes in with the pleasant days of May, parents mark with delight the physical developments of a year. They see broadening chests, rosy cheeks, clear eyes, tense muscles, pink skins, and bodies as hard as nails. Gone into thin air is the awkward, shambling walk, and instead there is an upright, well-balanced —not automatic — carriage, and a swinging gait nearly akin to the rhythmic suppleness which has made the marching of New York's Seventh Regiment famous everywhere.

Examinations are soon over, the graduating class goes out into the service for its professional course afloat, shore duty ends, and the new third-class man begins his two months' busy life on shipboard.

IX

"SIR," said Dr. Johnson, "no man will be a sailor who
has contrivance enough to get himself into jail;" and,
"Sir," undauntedly answers the youngster, with his first
practice cruise still unsailed—"sir, what an awful hum-
bug you can be sometimes." In the academy world this
initiatory cruise is eagerly expected by the cadet who
entered eight months before, because his surroundings
have magnified its mysteries, and given no little self-im-
portance to those who have made, if not the deep-water
voyages of the old days, at least the run between the
capes of Virginia and the Isles of Shoals.

Curiously enough, the academy's first practice-vessel
was a steamer, the *John Hancock*, though in the same
summer of 1851 the midshipmen cruised at sea and off
the coast of Maine in the sloop of war *Preble*. Before the
school was reorganized in that year, the course had been
always interrupted half-way by an obligatory three years'
service at sea in a cruising ship of war; but as this dissipated the benefits of instruction before habits of study
were formed, a curriculum extending through four suc-
cessive years, with an annual practice cruise, was adopted.
Since 1851 cruises have never been omitted, except in the
first year of the war, when the academy was moved to
Newport. From the modest beginning with the *John
Hancock* the value of the sea-work was found to be so
great, and the corps had so much increased, that the midshipmen, during and for some years after the war, cruised

not in a single ship, as at present, but in a squadron.
One of these—that of 1866, if I remember correctly—was
composed of seven vessels—three sailing-ships (two frigates and one sloop of war), three steamers, and the
schooner *America*. It is not generally known that this
famous yacht was captured in the St. John's River, about
1862, by the present Rear-Admiral T. H. Stevens (retired),
and that his officers and crew voluntarily offered to re-
sign all claims for prize-money upon the condition that
the schooner would be sent as a practice-vessel to the
Naval Academy. This promise was given and for some
years kept; but in 1873, in defiance of decency and justice, the yacht was put up at auction by the government
and sold for $5000, not a penny of which—to make the
whole affair more dishonorable, if possible — was ever
given to the blue-jackets, who were entitled to half the
prize value.

Other famous ships have been stationed at the academy, among them, and always first in the hearts of Amer-
icans, the *Constitution* of glorious memory. Here, also,
was stationed the *Macedonian*, captured in 1812 from the
British by the frigate *United States*, Captain Stephen De-
catur commanding; and for years the cadets cruised along
the coast in the *Constellation*, that renowned war-ship
which, under command of Commodore Thomas Truxton,
gallantly fought and defeated the frigates *L'Insurgente*
and *La Vengeance*, in our "quasi war" with France. There
is inspiration in the very names of these old warriors; and
so long as copper bolts and locust trunnels will hold live-
oak together, such of these ships as have not been sold
ought to be kept at Annapolis.

As soon as the first and third classes and all the new
appointments report on board the steamer *Bancroft* or
the sailing-ship assigned for the duty with their bags and

AN EARLY BATH

hammocks, they take up a routine which considers them purely and simply as man-o'-war's men. They are stationed, berthed, and messed as if in cruising ships, the first-class men being divided into weekly details, the duties of which differ widely. In one group they act as officers of the forecastle, tops, gangway, and quarter-deck, and as mates of decks; in the other they are rated as petty officers and seamen. The junior-class men are divided into watches, and distributed as forecastle men, fore, main, and mizzentop men, and after-guards; they pull the boats, man the gear, handle the sails, take the wheel, keep watch-and-watch at sea, stand lookout, and, indeed, perform all the duties, except cleaning ship, of the enlisted blue-jackets in the service. The regular crew of eighty-odd man the starboard battery, the cadets the port battery; but in pulling and hauling about decks the general work is done together.

The first night on board is still mildly exciting for the new appointments, but not as it was in the old days before "hazing," which is generally silly, often barbarous, and always useless, was stamped out.

Within a few days the cadets shake easily into their places, and by going over the mast-head every morning, sending up and down the light spars, and giving a pull here and a pull there and a long pull altogether everywhere for the best part of their waking hours, the youngsters soon acquire a nautical air and a fairly good grip upon the strange surroundings. Two or three days later the practice-ship drops down the Annapolis Roads, stands into Chesapeake Bay, and the long-looked-for cruise begins. Practical work commences at once, and if the winds be unfavorable, and they are usually, the ship beats down the bay in the daytime, and anchors at sunset. Here the new cadet sees the envied senior-class men in charge of

the deck, make and take in sail, tack, wear, boxhaul, and
chapel ship; sees him occasionally miss stays and box her
off, heave to, get casts of the deep-sea lead, shift sails and
spars, reef and shake out reefs, and bring the ship to an
anchor. All this time he is doing yeoman's service himself; his hands get horny and hard; his white working
clothes are tarry, and he is so used to "stamping and
going it" that when night comes he is glad to turn in
early, and leave the hardships of anchor watch to those
who have enjoyed the triumphs of the quarter-deck.
After Hampton Roads is reached, the vessel lies at
anchor for a week or more; but this is a busy season, and
all day long there are great-gun, company, pistol, or small-
arm drills, fire quarters, boats armed and equipped, or that
stirring exercise when the crew and cadets are called to
"abandon ship." This drill is usually executed without
previous warning, exactly as it might be needed in any
sudden emergency, as in a collision or danger of founder-
ing on the high sea; but within a moment after the order
rings out every one is at his station; some lower the
boats, others stand sentry over the falls, so no unauthorized or panic-stricken person may enter without orders;
the majority pass up provisions and water, cooking uten-
sils, arms, ammunition, and nautical instruments; there is
heard everywhere the rush of feet, the whimper of boat-
falls as the davits creak and complain with the strain and
the weight of the crews lowering themselves by stopper
or halyards. From every gun-port willing hands pass
stores into the cutters, and when ready each reports its
name and number. In less than five minutes, if the discipline be good, the crew is embarked in cutters, whalers,
launches, gig, and dingy, all submerged almost to their
gunwales, and the ship is abandoned—officially.

The distant, unvisited delights of Fortress Monroe are

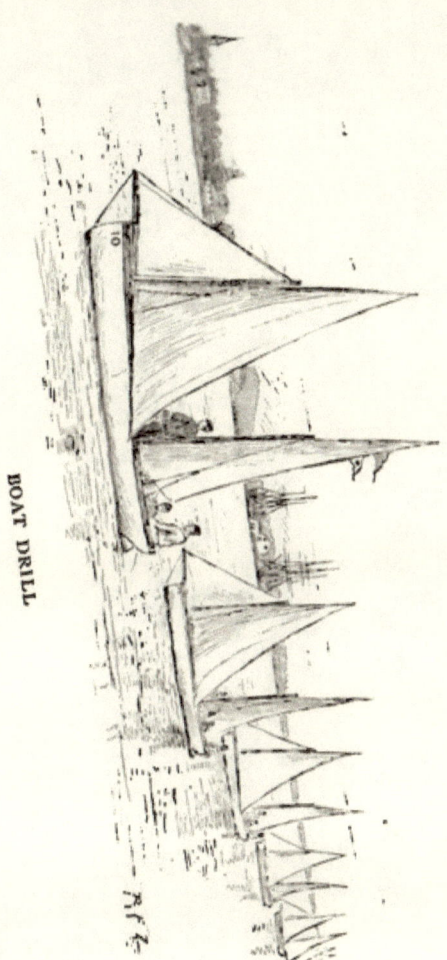

BOAT DRILL

soon left behind. The ship runs down the Roads with a free and a gallant wind, let us hope ; a departure is taken from the Capes, and the ship stands seaward. For the most part, cruises are made to the northward and eastward, sometimes in Long Island Sound and Gardiner's and Buzzard's bays, and always for some part of the time between Nantucket and the western limits of the Gulf Stream. All varieties of weather are taken as they come, not dodged ; and during the cruise the cadets are pretty sure to experience a fair share of gales, of heavy squalls, of flat calms, when the ship rolls helplessly on a sea gleaming like a shield of molten lead, of brisk breezes, of golden summer days, and star - lit nights. New London, Newport, or Portsmouth is visited, and a brief liberty given. And it is a delight to watch these youngsters enjoying a run ashore with all the zest of John Oxenham and Salvation Yeo, when, newly landed, these hearts of oak roared on Bideford Quay to the lads of Devon the merry catch of

"Westward ho ! with a rumbelow,
And hurrah for the Spanish Main, O !"

In addition to the usual exercises, and to the demands made by the exigencies of weather upon a sailing-ship, a course of instruction is regularly carried out. This is rigorously progressive, and includes practical work in seamanship, navigation, and gunnery.

The practice-ship sails slowly southward early in August, and arrives in Chesapeake Bay about the 15th. There is generally an exercise at carrying out anchors and clearing hawse in Lynn Haven Bay, and a sail and boat drill off Fortress Monroe; and the monotony of the cruise is invariably broken here by the long-expected ball given at the Hygeia Hotel. Slowly the last weeks come and go ; and a very happy day is it, indeed, when the ship picks

7

up her old anchorage in the inner harbor of Annapolis, and the first, second, and third class men go on leave for a month.

And by no one is this leave more appreciated or better deserved than by the second-class men. During the cruise they have lived on board the *Santee*, and have been given practical work in the machine - shop; in running steam-cutters; in target practice, afloat and ashore, with howitzers, machine pieces, and great guns; in boat drill, sail, and steam tactics, and in signalling with the navy and the army codes. Many hours of this time were spent at the work-benches of the steam-engineering building or in running the shop engines, and when the 1st of September gives them a well-earned holiday, they have something more than a rough acquaintance with workshop tools and appliances.

The youngster is now a proud third-class man; now a second; and almost before he begins to realize his dignity and honor in academy ways, his graduating day has come. The Board of Visitors—those potent, grave, and reverend seigniors, selected from the navy, from both Houses of Congress, and from civil life—have heard him recite, have seen him drill, have looked wise and overburdened with the weight of responsibility, and have written the capital report, which is so complimentary, so frank, and so full of recommendations that are [worse luck] rarely read and seldom adopted. Our happy youth has won the company flag, for he is, of course, a ranking cadet officer, and has worked hard to make his division victor in this traditional competition. Then comes the solemn hour. His cheeks are flushed; his heart beats intermittently; he listens to the long address, hears his name, catches the loud roar of applause—his own division loudest, most earnest of all—receives his diploma, and his school-days are over—his world is all before him.

SUPERSTITIONS OF THE SAILOR

SUPERSTITIONS OF THE SAILOR

I

A FEW lustrums have ebbed since the United States
sloop of war *Resaca* was employed upon the Pacific side
in that optimistic survey of the Isthmus of Panama which
was to reveal a tide-water canal route from ocean to
ocean. I was attached to the ship at this time—"very
much attached," as we all growled—and, like the others,
found the climate villanous, the work rigorous, the surroundings most depressing. Even in the preliminary
stages so many denials had to be enforced that at last, as
a concession to the civilized side of the men engaged
in the labor, an opportunity was offered them to send
home and receive letters through agencies less uncertain
than the pestilent bungoes which traded coastward from
the Gulf of San Miguel. Into these denials entered many
essentials, such as clean linen and mess stores, so when
it was announced that the sailing-launch, adequately
equipped and manned, was to go to Panama, there were
arrayed such a mail, personal and official, and such lists of
stores necessary for the successful pursuit of the elusive
routes, that the departure of the craft took on a fine air of
ceremonious congratulation. When the boat shoved clear of
the ship's side, the men crowding the rail, and the officers

gathered aft, sped her in a hearty cheer the warmest of
God-speeds; the ship's dog barked, the landsmen swore
at their bondage, and the forecastle cat glared silently
from the pivot-port. For hers was an absorbing interest,
as among the launch's crew was that very tender-hearted
blue-jacket whose affection for the cat had made him go
the length of sporting her tattooed portrait, in the pri-
mary colors so dear to Jacky, upon a stalwart forearm,
where a very weeping-willow and an impossible tomb
divided the muscles with a quaint distich out of a sailor's
hornbook.

The cat gazed long and uncannily from the pivot-port
rail, her tail waving a protesting adieu, and her whiskers
rigged out with the rigidity of a Greek brig's bowsprit.
When the boat turned a bend in the river, and was shut
in by a lush fringe of mangrove, the cat jumped spitefully
to the deck, walked forward (back arched and tail swollen,
like a magnified frankfurter), spat at the yellow dog we
had—conveyed, the wise call it—up-river, and then disappeared—forever.

Whether she dropped overboard in the swift tide-
stream of the Tuyra, or was astrally translated, none of
us ever learned after the closest inquest; but that surely
was the end of cat number one, as we despairingly called
her.

Two nights afterwards, when in-shore, fairly well up
Panama way, the launch, spitted by a squall from no-
man's-land, turned turtle, belched mail, and coin, and
linen, and all the rest of it, to the sharks, and one man,
the cat's particular adoption, was drowned.

Six months later, and after a deal of trying work, the
Resaca gained a well-earned anchorage off the murky
coast of Callao. Here we met an American, a civil engineer of exceeding promise, who was engaged as chief of

division in the survey of that cloud-assailing route which started from Lima, skirted the Rimac, and then zigzagged over the hills at an elevation deadly to the plain-reared gringo. He was low in his clever mind, hipped, sapped by fever and anxieties, and pathetically hungry for home and American faces and ways. We stumbled into his story through a lucky pitfall, though this may have no place here. It opened our hearts, however, for he was a stranger in a freebooting zone, and we were his country-men, and surely that was enough to make the mess beg him to come on board for a chance at the sea breezes and a sure hit at American ways and faces.

The night he crawled over the gangway the ship's new cat slipped overboard, but with such pitiful mewings and clawings that the rush of rescuers nearly swamped the lowered boat. By the flare of signal torches and deck lanterns Tom was seen in the nick of time, and to every-body's content was hauled safely inboard.

Our visitor found a tonic in the breeze and the rest and novelty of the life; he made a most receptive target for the mess-worn stories, and all around proved such a good sort of American that when, ten days later, he announced his intention of striking the beach for the afternoon, a howl of growls went up, which had a sane echo in the calm and strong protest of the surgeon. It seemed, how-ever, that he had to go, for one of his inventions, upon which depended the immediate support of his old people at home, was then under examination by the authorities.

He remained ashore after sundown, came off in the damp boat of a drunken fletero, who raised a row half-way to the ship about the fare, and when he climbed the gang-way was so worn out with the running about and heat and worry that he had to be helped to his state-room. Just as two bells struck in the first watch (nine at night),

and tattoo had its echo in taps beaten, the doctor came on
deck to tell us that the engineer was in a bad way; but
in the middle of his explanations we heard a scramble on
the housed awning, saw a tangle of flying feet and claw-
ing paws, and heard a splash, a wailing mew of despair,
answered by the bleat of a belated seal paddling towards
San Lorenzo, seaward. Cat number two was overboard,
this time for good and all: for though the nearest boat
went into the water by the run, and willing fingers gripped
oar-looms and handles, it was too late. The cat had
slipped into the darkness, and was borne shoreward on the
flood, surging riotously.

When the ebb was making, about two in the morning
of the second day, the young engineer stretched out a
faltering hand to the doctor and to the rest of us gathered about him, tried to tell us something about his inven-
tion, and died.

After long days at sea, and longer ones in stunted
Peruvian and Chilian ports, the *Resaca* anchored one
breezy morning off the town of Talcahuano, which offers
such large possibilities to sailors. Here some one was
given a wonderful kitten, yellow and gray, with curious
interlacings of black and tawny rings. It was a breed
strange to the country, so everybody said, and no one pre-
tended to account for it save Lafferty, a Californian, who
ran the Fourth of July Hotel. This tavern was much fre-
quented by sailors of all degrees, and here one day, in the
captain's room, religiously tabooed to all save master-
mariners and naval officers, Lafferty told in an ornamental
lie how the kitten's mother had appeared suddenly after
a rainfall, and how she proved to be, not a Dago cat, but
one of an Indian breed, born on the silent, yellow pampas, which stretched over the hills for miles and miles out
Argentine way.

The kitten grew into a very gentle cat, took kindly to all hands, though it adopted as its special ward the senior watch-officer, who, by-the-way, was the only man in the mess that had a wife and baby to keep him out of mischief.

Those were busy days for the ship off that nook-shotten coast, and so after another six months the *Resaca* was one morning at sea, standing up the shore, bound for Payta, when the senior watch-officer came on deck and learned that the cat was dead. In a mad chase after a rat diving into a chain-pipe, it had made a jump from the topgallant forecastle, struck its head on the cable, and ended thus untimely its career. After his manner, the senior watch-officer fell into sad forebodings. When the day broke, the gear was laid up, decks were swept, and preparations made for washing down. Hardly had the hickory brooms begun their swishing when White—John White, captain of the starboard watch of the after-guard —staggered against the bulwarks, and said, " I feel bad, sir," and then gripping his throat, continued, "all throttled here." Two hands were ordered to help White forward, the doctor was called, the apothecary aroused.

Just as the gray dawn silvered into a clear day the doctor came—in pajamas—with a leap and a bound on deck, asked what the row was, and started forward ; but in the centre of a silent crowd of sailors of the watch gathered at the weather-gangway he stopped. It was too late ; White was dead.

After the captain of the after-guard had been buried, and the ship had gathered way on her old course northward, the petty officers came to the mast, and asked to see the captain. When he appeared, the senior sailorman, cap in hand, forelock properly patted, spoke up manfully and quietly. The burden of his request—this most

gravely considered, most earnestly granted—was that the
ship's company begged that no more cats be allowed on
board.   He went on to prove that they brought bad luck,
black cats and strange, foreign cats especially, and while
the people forward were not superstitious, still queer
things had happened of late, and he felt it to be only fair
that the captain should know how the men looked at it.

Lafferty's pampas cat was the last we shipped that
cruise, and the rats had a fine run of the holds thereafter,
until one day Bill Clarke, late champion light-weight of
South Australia, and then proprietor of a snug English
pub and dog-pit in Callao, came off to the ship by con-
tract, and, baiting his traps with melon rinds, caught in
two nights more rats than may be chronicled here.

This, of course, is an over-long yarn to reel off in order
to prove that superstition is still foolishly potent with
sailors.   It is as easy as fudging a day's work to show
that, in the case quoted, coincidences were mistaken for
causes, and that the evidence needed a link or two ; but it
was another curious coincidence that no more men died
suddenly that cruise after we gave up enlisting cats.

WATER-LOGGED

II

AFTER studying them fairly well, I doubt if modern sailors are more superstitious than any other class with equal training and opportunities. I believe that everybody is leavened with superstition, notably the noisiest scoffers, and those mountebanks, the Thirteen Clubs, for these gentry protest too much. It seems to be a human instinct, modified by racial inheritances and developments. In the youth of the world its manifestations were the earliest recorded utterances of men concerning the visible phenomena of the universe, and its grip on simple minds was an outgrowth of the fear of the unknown. Of all people sailors must deal at first hand, and helplessly to some degree, with the most unknowable, uncontrollable of material problems, the sea, and it is only natural that their folk-lore should be, in part, land stories fitted with sea meanings, and, in part, blind explanations of sea phenomena — both being maintained valorously by the grewsome conservatism of the seaman, even after rational causes come to the rescue.

In earlier days superstition was as much a part of every ship as the water she was to float in; for it entered with the wood scarfed into her keel, and climbed to the flags and garlands waving at her mast-heads; it ran riotously at her launching, controlled her name, her crew, and cargoes; it timed her days and hours of sailing, and convoyed her voyages. It summoned apparitions for her ill fortune, and evoked portents and signs for her prosperity; it made

winds blow foul or fair, governed her successful ventures
and arrivals, and, when her work was done, promised a
port of rest somewhere off the shores of Fiddler's Green,
where all good sailors rest eternally, or threatened foul
moorings deep in the uncanny locker of Davy Jones of
ballad memory.

In many countries stolen wood was mortised into the
keel, as it made the ship sail faster at night; though if the
first blow struck in fashioning this keel drew fire, the ship
was doomed to wreck upon her maiden voyage. Silver
(usually a coin) placed in the mainmast-step went for
lucky ventures, and misguided indeed was the owner who
permitted any of the unlucky timbers to enter into the
construction. Something of the ceremonious character
given to launchings survives to this day: where, of old,
ships were decked with flowers and crowns of leaves,
flags now flutter; the libation poured on the deck, the
purification by the priest, the anointing with egg and
sulphur, find their exemplars in the well-aimed and wasted
magnums which are shattered on the receding cut-water as
the craft, released from the ways, slips, well greased, into
the sea; the jar of wine put to his lips by the captain and
then emptied on deck, the cakes and ale set before the
crew, the stoup of wine offered to passers-by on the quay,
and the refusal of which was an evil omen — all are realized in these sadder lustrums by the builder's feast in the
mould-loft.

Lawyers, clergymen, and women are ever looked at
with disfavor on sailing-ships as sure to bring ill luck—
lawyers, undoubtedly, from the antipathy of sailors to the
class, a dislike so pronounced that "sea-lawyer" is a very
bitter term of reproach, and "land-shark" is a synonyme.
Clergymen — priests and parsons — are unlucky, probably
because of their black gowns and their principal duty on

shipboard—that of consoling the dying and burying the dead—though possibly because the devil, the great storm-raiser, is their especial enemy, and sends tempests to destroy them. Women—who may reason out their unpopularity? save that a ship is the last place for them, or perhaps because of the dread of witches; for of all spell-workers in human form none is so dreaded as the female brewers of hell-broth. Like the priests of the Middle Ages, they can raise a prime quality of storm by tossing sand or stones in the air, and, like Congreve's Lapland sorceress, are supposed to live by selling contrary winds and wrecked vessels.

Russian Fins—or "Roosian" Fins, as Jacky has it—were, and are yet, wizards of high degree. Hurricanes blew, calms beset, gales roared, as they willed, and their incantations began to operate by the simple sticking of a knife in the mast. If they wished to drive the rats out of a vessel, they shoved the point of a snickersnee into the deck, and every rat ran for the sharp blade, and willy-nilly performed *hara-kiri*. No one ever saw, in sailor lore, a penniless Russian Fin, for by slipping his hand into his pocket he can always produce a gold doubloon—why a gold doubloon no one seems to know, but it is always that coin; his rum-bottle, often consulted silently and alone, is never full nor empty—a gentle plashing of tide-half-tide bringing fat content, and woe be to the incautious mariner who bites the weather-side of his thumb at His High Nobility the spell-worker, for harm will surely follow.

Certain families could never get sea employment under their own surnames, not even such members as were born with cauls, for they were tabooed, barred; and many animals—hares, pigs, and black cats, for example—could neither be carried nor mentioned on shipboard, save under very stringent conditions.   Scarborough wives kept a black cat in the house to assure their husbands' lives at sea; but on voyages every black cat carried a gale in her tail, and if she became unusually frolicsome a storm was sure to follow.   Years ago, on board the flag-ship *Franklin*, up the Mediterranean, we had a yarn that illustrated a survival of this antipathy to certain forms of animal life. Two old quartermasters were heard during the morning watch exchanging in the cockpit dismal experiences of their dreams the night before.   One was particularly harrowing, for the narrator wound up with, "And I say, Bill, I was never so afeared in my life; when I woke up it seemed as true as day, and I was all of a tremble like an *asp on a leaf.*"

"What's that?" said the other.   "Pipe down; don't mention that rep-tile; he's a hoodoo on shipboard."

Whistling—and let us honor this sweet tradition—is very much against the proprieties of sea-life. You may, in a calm, if not a landsman, woo with soothing whistle San Antonio or Saint Nicholas, and a lagging wind may be spurred in consequence by these patron saints of the mariner; but once the ship is going, never, wise and wary passenger, whistle, if you fear keel-hauling, for, like the Padrone in the "Golden Legend," you may find

> "Only a little while ago,
> I was whistling to Saint Antonio
> For a capful of wind to fill our sail,
> And instead of a breeze he has sent a gale."

Figure-heads were at first images of gods, and later of saints and sea-heroes, and were held in high reverence. To this hour the eyes glaring from the bow of a Chinese junk enable the boat to voyage intelligently — for "no have two eyes, how can see? No can see, how can

do?" is the shibboleth of their sailors. Ships' bells were
blessed, and to-day if a mistake in their striking is made
by a stupid messenger-boy, they are struck backward to
break the spell.   In one ship to which I was attached the
bell had come down to us from the *Ticonderoga*, through
the *Thetis*, I think, and was supposed to be under the
special control of a blue spirit of mischief. Why the
blue spirit should indulge in such vagaries is hidden, but
in the middle of deep - sea nights, when the moon rode in
an auspicious quarter, and the wind blew with the force
and from the direction necessary for the spell, the blue
bell was bound to make a complete circle, and ring out
nine bells stridently. Of course no one ever heard or
ought to hear nine bells at sea, for eight bells are as
fixed in limit as the decalogue; but this was promised.
Whether the conditions failed to co-ordinate I cannot
say, but though the bell was watched by all sorts and
conditions of men, the occult ceremony was never performed for our benefit. Is it necessary to add that by
report it was a common event in the other ships mentioned?

The proverbial desertion of sinking ships by rats is
founded upon reason, and undoubtedly occurs, for as rats
like to prowl about dry-footed, and will stick to one place
so long as food is plenty, it is probable that the ship they
leave is so leaky and unseaworthy that their underdeck
work is too wet to suit them.

Most of the ceremonies of ship-life are of long descent,
but, I believe, none is more ancient nor more honored in
the observance than those attendant upon crossing the
line, whether it be the equator with deep-water ships or
the arctic circle with whalers. The details of the performance vary even among the ships of the same waters;
but it is always a tribute to Neptune exacted of the offi-

cers, crew, and passengers new to the waters entered. Bassett gives a description, taken from Marryat's *Frank Mildmay*, which is true of our ships in essentials. With us the ship is usually hailed from the supposed depths of the sea the evening before the line is to be reached, and the captain is given the compliments of Neptune, and asked to muster his novices for the sea-lord's inspection. The next day the ship is hove to at the proper moment, and Neptune, with his dear Amphitrite and suite, comes on board over the bow or through a bridle-port, if the weather permits.

"Neptune appears [writes Marryat] preceded by a young man, dandily dressed in tights and riding on a car made of a gun-carriage drawn by six nearly naked blacks, spotted with yellow paint. He has a long beard of oakum, an iron crown on his head, and carries a trident with a small dolphin between its prongs. His attendants consist of a secretary with quills of the sea-fowl; a surgeon with lancet and pill-box; a barber with a huge wooden razor, with its blade made of an iron hoop, and a barber's mate, with a tub for a shaving-box. Amphitrite, wearing a woman's nightcap with sea-weed ribbons on her head, and bearing an albacore on a harpoon, carries a ship's boy in her lap as a baby, with a marlinspike to cut his teeth on. She is attended by three men dressed as nymphs, with currycombs, mirrors, and pots of paint. The sheep-pen, lined with canvas and filled with water, has already been prepared. The victim, seated on a platform laid over it, is blindfolded, then shaved by the barber, and finally plunged backward into the water. Officers escape by paying a fine in money or rum."

To this day it is the roughest sort of rough man-handling, but it is a short shrift for those who take it good-naturedly, and, like bear-baiting, affords great amusement to the spectators.

On Good Friday, in many ports, Roman Catholic sailors cockbill their yards, slack their gear, and scourge Judas, as signs of mourning. In the harbor of New York I have

CROSSING THE LINE—INITIATING A DEEP-WATER SAILOR

seen the effigy of Judas hanged to a yard-arm until sunset, then lowered, and so belabored and beaten, so cuffed
and kicked, that it seemed a mercy when it was burned to
a charred mass in the galley, and the ashes were scattered
with contumely on the water. Spanish sailors, on certain
days of the week or month, lay aloft at sunset, and beat
the sheaves and pins of the blocks—pulleys, as shore people call them. This is driving the devil out of the gear,
and a fine din it makes, for the Spaniards put their brawn
into it. After all, it is nothing more than a general order
popularized, and is the result of a certain disaster, when a
Spanish squadron, surprised at a long-occupied anchorage,
could not make sail to engage the enemy because the pins
and sheaves of all the principal blocks had rusted in their
seatings.

Nothing was more common at sea in the old days than
apparitions, from horned and monstrous seamen, through
saints and red-bearded Norse gods, to that dreadful spec-
tre of the Cape, Adamastor, who is sometimes seen even
yet, in the twilight, hovering in cloud and mist over the
white folds of the Devil's Table-cloth mantling the head-
land of Good Hope. More picturesque than any other,
perhaps, is the Flying Dutchman, whose tale is told with
variations in nearly every maritime country, and whose
sad mishaps have formed the burden of many a song and
story. Jal gives the accepted version thus:

"An unbelieving Dutch captain had vainly tried to round Cape
Horn against a head gale. He swore he would do it, and when the
gale increased, laughed at the fears of his crew, smoked his pipe,
and drank his beer. He threw overboard some of the crew who
tried to make him seek a port. The Holy Ghost descended upon
the vessel, but, firing his pistol at the apparition, he pierced his
own hand and paralyzed his arm. He cursed God, and was then
condemned to navigate always without putting into port; only

8

having gall to drink, and red-hot iron to eat, and a watch to keep
that should last forever. He was to be the evil genius of the sea,
to torment Spanish sailors; the sight of his storm-tossed bark to
carry presage of ill-fortune to luckless beholders. He sends white
squalls, disasters, tempests. Should he visit a ship, wine sours,
and all food becomes beans; should he bring or send letters they
must not be touched on pain of death and damnation. His crew are
all old sinners of the sea, sailor thieves, cowards, and murderers,
who suffer and toil eternally, and have little to eat and less to drink."

Cooper tells us that the vessel is said to be a double-
decker, seen always to windward, sometimes half hidden
during clear weather, often under all sail in a gale, and on
occasions veering and hauling among the clouds. The
ship's history has been chronicled with the particularity of
a great war, and in the late Lieutenant Bassett's book
many curious particulars of her woful fate and of her
Heaven-cursed skipper will be found.

To the adventurous globe-trotter who has climbed the
rock-path to the sailors' church of Notre Dame de la
Garde, dominating the Phenician port of Marseilles, the
potent influence of sacrifices and offerings for perils passed
and to come must be no old story. There is a pathos,
even for the worldly, in the quaint ships and galleons,
in the rusting marline-spikes and shattered tiller-heads,
swinging to the mistral, in reverential offering before
the shrines. These graces after danger, these insurances
against evil to come, circle the world. No people have
escaped the influence of such hopes and thanks. Our Indians were fettered by them, and no ceremonious offerings
were more common than those which went to appease
the angry Spirit of the Waters. On the upper tributaries
of the Mississippi, the Indians, with occult rites, gave
tribute of tobacco from a beetling cliff to the Great Spirit
of the River, and to the winds that smote the waters with

FLOGGING JUDAS

blasts from the caverns of the jealous gods. Algonquins
in the North, Aztecs, sons of Atahualpa and Manco Capac,
in the South—all blew incense out of their pipes, and
strewed upon the currents and tideways just such offerings of tobacco as, in our more subjective days, we give
with lost meanings to the minor gods who rule the man's
hour in our feasts.

But not alone did apparitions, or votive offerings which
must be made, crowd to daunt the sailor, for in his voyages ghostly lights would gleam suddenly from yard-arms
or mast-heads, and at the bowsprit-cap spectral flames might
cast weird reflections upon the water.

> "High on the mast, with pale and lurid rays,
> Amid the gloom portentous meteors blaze,"

is the manner in which Falconer sang of it, though among
the Latin seafaring races the St. Elmo's Fire or the cor-
posant is, especially if seen double, the best of omens, and
is hailed as evidence of Heaven's care for ship and crew.
Dampier described it as a small, glittering light, like a star
when it shines at the mast-head, like a glowworm when it
appears on deck. He believed it to be some kind of a
jelly, but we know now that it is an electrical discharge,
which occurs in rarefied conditions of the atmosphere, and
adheres to the iron of the spars, as the metal is the best
conductor available.

Many modern sailors will reject this explanation as in-
complete, and in the older days it would have been scoffed
at, and banned by bell, book, and candle, for it was one of
the commonest and most cherished of superstitions held
by the men who went down to the sea in ships and saw
the supernatural everywhere.

THE BASKET OF THE SEA

THE BASKET OF THE SEA

I

IF anything ought to have reconciled the crew of the *Resaca*, sloop of war, to the prospect of a nine-months' cruise among the trade-wind islands of the Pacific—isolated as they were to be from newspapers, shore grub, and home letters, indeed from all that makes the civilization of sailors—it should have been the glorious weather blessing the first month of the voyage. Beautiful days and starry nights encircled the run, and its log recorded blithe memoranda of blue waters, bright skies, and honest breezes. Steadily westward the ship slipped over the tropical seas, her port stunsails bellying alow and aloft in the daylight, plain sail to to'-gallant sails holding after sundown, and, for a mariner's merry merry-making all work, save drills, beginning and ending with an occasional pull here and a pull there on sheets and tacks and halyards. Not an hour of gale roared, not a bucket of rain fell— "old woman's weather," the blue-jackets called it—a sea-going as dry as remainder biscuit after voyage, and without a prophecy of that other sailorizing which later they were to know in the roaring Forties.

Twenty-eight days after the headlands of San Lorenzo were lost in the mists of Callao Bay the ship reached the eastern edge of the treacherous Paumotus; and when "Land ho!" rang from the mast-head lookout, eager eyes

saw two isolated clumps of palm-trees lifting their trunks
and branches, seemingly, out from the depths of an ocean
which no lead had sounded. At their distance from the
ship the fringe of low reef and the spit of coral were
shrouded by the horizon, and it needed an unquestioning
faith in the sines and cosines of the Navigator, fortified
by the hard - and - fast facts of the sailing directions, to
make these spectral trees anything but delusions of the
place and season. When they dipped below the verge
sternward new islets lifted their welcoming groves, these
atolls being often frail rings of coral, raised but a few feet
above the sea, and cut, where the prevailing currents bat-
tered steadily, into channel-ways, through which the long
rollers surged brokenly. For forty-eight hours more the
ship ran through uncharted tide - streams past other islands; and then, just after one bell in the morning watch
of a day in June, a little flare of light, hanging steadfastly
over the great Pacific billows, punctuated the graying
darkness of the morning. It was too low for a star, too
steady for a light afloat, but it grew and grew until at
last, just before the day broke, it blossomed into the
promise that Point Venus of Tahiti—the Nouvelle Cy-
thére of Bouganville—was waiting dead ahead, as the
course was shaped.

The morning dawned sullenly, with such a diffusion of
grayish tints and such a sluggish uprising of the sun that
the island seemed more a ghostly shape wreathed in mist
than the earthly paradise the early voyagers had pictured.
Its precipitous summits towered over harsh gorges, and
its gray sides frowned as aridly as the mountains dominating the narrow shorelands of Chili and Peru. As the
day marched other islands stole out of the sea, some showing the tips of fantastic peaks and others silhouetting their
sharp outlines against a background of clearing sky. By-

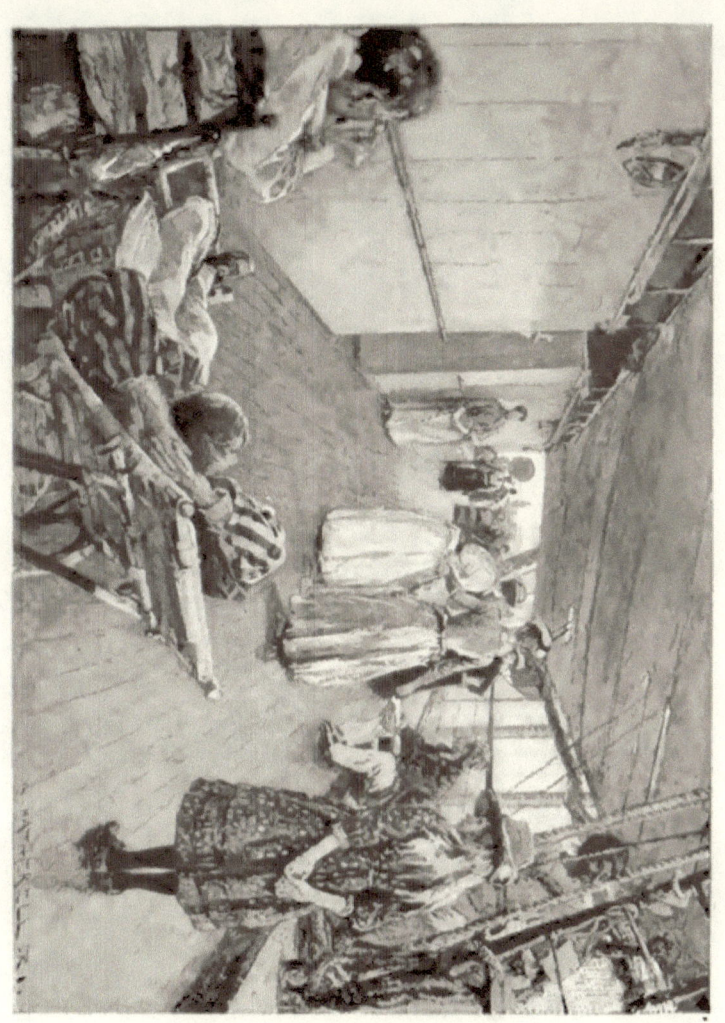

and-by the wind freshened, and as the *Resaca* rushed landward before a brave to'gallant breeze glints and gleams
warmed the upper sky.   Then the sunshine sought slowly
the steep ridges of the island, bathing peak and pinnacle
in a flood of gold, and then it crept shoreward with a
slow enfolding that glorified the foot-hills and the slopes.

The pilot, beaming with a thousand welcomes, awaited
clear of the barrier reef ; and when he had guided the ship
through the coral gates and shot her, under top-sails, jib,
and spanker, into the choicest anchorage of the harbor,
he took off his cap, and with his finest bow welcomed
everybody to "the garden-spot of the world—to Papeeté."

"And Papeeté means?—" asked the navigator.

"'The Basket of the Sea.'"

II

SEEN from the anchorage, Tahiti justified its traditions and its sailor poets. It was a fairy vision of the sea, a realization of the rapturous descriptions which glow in the narratives of Prince Leboo and of those other navigators who sang its glories in quaint and ardent phrases years ago. Its beauty, really measureless by words, was far beyond the high praise of Quoy, of Lesson, of Dumont d'Urville, far beyond even that fervid appreciation which the pen, usually so sober, of Captain Cook set down in the pages of his Discoveries.

The town lay in a narrow plain that curved with the shore, and was bedded in groves of bread-fruit, pandanus, and palm. Jasmine and crimson hibiscus accentuated the greenness of hill-sides dotted with huts, which clung to buttresses of trellised rock or hid beside crystal lakes that hurried a hundred streams shoreward. The upper hills, green with the broad leaves of the "faie"—the native plantain—rose through terraces and crags into Ovethena, seven thousand feet above the sea.

At the east and west cusps of the crescent beach Fareúte and Hotanéa Points closed the land view, while seaward the billowing expanse was broken only by the rugged hills of Moorea and by the domes of Tetuarova.

Watched from the shore, the silence of the long, foamless rollers of the Pacific was awe-inspiring, and their hidden powers were revealed only when, in their westerly sweeping, they assaulted the coral barriers and rioted over

their walls in breakers booming thunderously. Within
the reef the waters were calm and still, and so clear that
the harbor's bed lay as an open book for your reading.

The cool streets were arched by trees interlaced so
thickly that the sunlight barely filtered in queer traceries
upon the turf, and everywhere was a fragrant and brilliant
shrubbery. The troops of natives thronging the beach
were mated to the scene. The women were tall, well
formed, and graceful, with every limb untrammelled by
the fetters of civilized dress; their gowns, long and of a
dear old fashion, and in color everything from red to
white, floated loosely in an unstudied harmony; their
hair, trailing negligently, was crowned with chaplets of
arroa-root or with the white and odorous reva-reva; and
their voices bubbled in the laughter of an age and season
where life was always play-time. The men, tall, firmly
built, and sure in carriage, were princes of the fairest of
fairy-lands, compared with the little, blustering Peruanos
left over the water, and their faces were as pleasant and
honest as an Easter-day. Their complexion, darker than
that of the Spaniards, was not so olive as with the higher
type of Moors, the men, if anything, being fairer than the
women. Nothing of the Papuan or negro showed in any
lineament, but well-developed Malay characteristics, recalling strongly the types that exist on those shores whence
drifted years ago the progenitors of the race; and their
eyes, black and mild, fairly sparkled with pleasure when
you were greeted, as you were always, with that merry
salutation, "Ya rana," which means so little and so much.

What a happy lot they seemed to be!—either so
blessed that life with them was a holiday, or so philo-
sophic that nothing could disturb their unruffled acceptance of the joys of the day; and let it be chronicled here
that in all our time among them they never failed in that

genuine good-nature and perfect courtesy which are among
the noblest characteristics of a race. Even the little children lisped a greeting; and to the poorest sailor that trod
the beach, or to the greatest swell for whom the harbor
guns blazed out a welcome, the same smile, the same in-
vitation to their huts, the perpetual and jocund "Ya rana"
were accorded.

The town of Papeeté is the largest in Tahiti—indeed,
it is the only one that may be dignified with that name.
One principal street traversed its length, and from this,
branching at varying angles and following the whim of
the earliest builders, streets and lanes straggled to the
beach or to the base of the mountains. Here, perhaps,
narrowed to some winding path, these crept upward to
the exterior fastnesses of the island, for there is no interior to the island—not in our sense, at least—and all
roads wound around, not over, the hills. The houses of
the foreigners faced the sea or the streets and lanes leading to it, and were built of wood in the American style.
They were well situated, cool, airy, and neat, with tempt-
ing verandas and enticing hammocks, and were surrounded by plants and trees, native and exotic. Here the aloe
and vanilla bloomed with the hibiscus and pandanus, or
with those others so long since acclimated as to be native
—the orange, the lime, and the banana. The level land
had an average breadth of half a mile from the shore
to the mountain spurs, though valleys extended this in
many places far up the sides of the hills. Down the
mountain brooks skylarked to the sea, but not until they
had worked through the coral barrier the many openings
which pierce the reef. Beyond and surrounding the town
were the native huts, built of hibiscus poles and wattled
with twigs, the roofs thatched with pandanus and the
walls plastered with coral lime. Groves of plantain and

bread-fruit sheltered them on the landward side, and from their door-steps foam-caps could be seen sporting in the sunlight. Nothing was allowed to shut off this sea view; for the Tahitian has a keen perception of beauty, and to him the blue ocean and the waving palm are necessities born of his nature.

The more pretentious residences are grouped to the eastward, and here were the government houses, the barracks, the arsenal, the palace, and the club, all fronting on the famous Broom or Purumu Road, which encircled the island, but which here rejoiced in the name of Rue de Rivoli. French influence was paramount everywhere, but in nothing more assertively than in the titles of the streets and buildings, the meanest alleys and the shabbiest structures revelling in names that recalled the noted thoroughfares of famous cities. About the centre of the town, and opposite the Rue de la Reine, was the palace of her late Majesty Queen Pomare IV.—a magnificent building for Tahiti, glorious in unfulfilled promises, and situated in mean though extensive grounds. Under its shadow crouched two or three little cabins, and here in undignified ease reposed her Majesty and her suite when it pleased her to visit the town.

The principal shops and the warehouses of the wealthier merchants fronted the beach, for trade was brisk with the Paumotus and the Leeward Islands, and many cargoes of oil and pearl shells were landed on the rickety jetties. At one time this business was of great extent, and generally pursued among the groups, but it appeared here to be engrossed by a few persons, who claimed its control lay in Tahiti. The principal import trade was with California, and in many of the shops the typical "toothpick to an anchor" stock might be found, and, what was better, with genuine Yankees to sell it. This trade was car-

ried on by sharp, well-built "Frisco schooners," that made
most wonderful runs outward, and found for homeward
cargoes delicious oranges that rivalled those of Malaga
and Seville. To them, also, the people were indebted for
their mail, and to minds hungering for news their coming
was as great a matter of moment as will be the arrival
of mail steamers when the necessities of coaling stations
make these islands take their proper strategic place in
the sea power of the world.

III

THE history of this group, from the year 1767, when Wallis anchored in the harbor of Matavai, to the assumption of the protectorate by Guizot, is a twice-told tale. Captain James Cook landed here to observe the transit of Venus, and, sailing northward and eastward, he discovered and revisited those islands and shores that will carry his fame to posterity as the Columbus of this ocean. Here the mutineers of the *Bounty* rested, and like very tarry and rough eighteenth-century lotus-eaters, here they revelled greedily until the prospect of capture and a short shrift sent them scurrying post-haste with their wives to more distant, if securer, shores. Bouganville, La Pérouse, Krusenstern, and Wilkes, among other sea-worthies, surveyed these waters. Here the missionaries, and later here the French, came, and then the buzzing tops of clashing interests began the spinning that wrecked the land. For the Polynesian world is divided upon the merits of these invaders, and the tales told by vituperative traders and beach-combers, and the stories handed down in native tradition, are no less difficult to reconcile with the truth than the sweeping denials made by Church and State. Here, later still, appeared the Jesuits and other missionaries of denominations at war with the original teachers, and then began in earnest that conflict of creed and race of which the echoes rumble yet. What is certain, evil came out of it all, for the heathens, who had at first willingly accepted everything taught by the white man, now found them-

selves between the devil and the deep sea of polemics.
They were forced to listen while their masters renewed
the world-tired battles of other lands; to hear a different
and an only God preached in orthodox fashion; to wan-
der confusedly through the subtleties of warring dogmas;
until at last, in sheer confusion as to old landmarks and
charted channel ways, they lost their reckoning and drifted
pilotlessly into the dead seas of sectarianism. In the end
they were forced to choose, and, as often as not, they gave
allegiance not from belief and acceptance, but from a
worldly admiration of the physically bigger teacher, or of
him, big or little, whose stores of carnal goods promised
better rewards.

The fight was intensified by the old antagonism of races,
of a Frenchman against a Briton, of a fiery religious Cra-
paud against an obstinately religious Johbool; and it was
imbittered by difference of cultures, of aims, of diverging interests, and commingling fanaticisms. Finally, from theses
and polemics the disputants resorted to force and threats
of extinction; and these, even to the regenerate, were no
easier to bear because they were clothed in sanctimoni-
ous phrase and pious invocation. In the end the priests
were condemned—bell, book, and candle—and expelled,
and under circumstances more galling than Exeter Hall
and the British Foreign Office would have the world believe. Finally, the Frenchman returned with his fleet, and
threatened with one noble broadside, after the approved
French manner—the grand manner, they call it—to blow
missionaries, heathens, towns, and churches down the idle
wind, and thus settle the affair forever. *Pourparlers,* pre-
texts, promises, intimidations, all the whimsical paper bul-
lets of the brain branded as diplomacy, followed; and
then, after "seizure of the royal person" (poor dusky
monarch) and bombardment, the curtain rose on the last

scene of all, when, with blare of trumpet, and thundering
of guns, and *vives* till the welkin rang, the French king,
who scarcely knew that such an oasis bloomed in the wa-
tery desert, seized upon the groups under the inspiring plea
of "protection." Possession followed in name years after,
but from that day to this, through good fortune and ill
and all the vicissitudes of the home government, Tahiti
remained a part of colonial France.

The usual British growl, the time - worn explanations
from the ministerial benches, the inevitable native revolu-
tion followed, but in vain, for by the grace of the French
government, Pomaré Vahine—Pomaré the woman—was
allowed to succeed and to rule as a puppet, whose strings
were pulled by courteous commandants. The tricolor
was deftly woven in the union of the Tahitian flag, and
in the still evenings, where the blast of the war conch or
the pleading harmony of the uté were wont to sound, the
fanfare of bugles echoing the fame of Père Bugeaud succeeded, recalling, perhaps, to the sensitive Tahitian mind,
if such exist, the faded glories of a race that had crumbled
beneath the wheels of civilization.

With this seizure by the French the political power of
the missionary died, and it died hard. Though their books
and reports described a golden age reborn, in which sub-
mission, domestic and religious, was based upon the fervor
of a race awakened to the highest truths, we know it was
a strong, a relentless governing. Good came out of it in
many ways, and yet not such unmixed good as settles at
this day the dispute which rule, that of the early missionary or that of the French, was the better. Making due
allowances for the prejudices which rankle, it is still a
vexed question, because there are no loci of agreement.
The first missionaries, were, as a rule, men of humble origin,
who could handle the jack-plane and the hammer more

9

deftly than the intricacies of the moral law. It was a time when the new regions entering the zone of man's knowledge were opening fields for an extension of the charity and humanity of the world's greatest religion. It was a season when many earnest but untrained men felt compelled to quit the guilds wherein they were adepts for the higher mission of teaching the heathen; to leave work wherein they had become skilled through infinite care and practice for other and more difficult labor, to which they brought no other qualities than honest hearts, sound bodies, and great intentions. It was a time, too, when men of this class, stirred to their hearts by the bidding of the gentle Master, were apt from biassed thought and half-awakened perceptions to behold a mission, and perhaps deluded by their wordy gift of "wagging a pow i' the pulpit," to believe themselves foreordained to convert the heathen. The fallow field was waiting, and often the societies demanded little more than fixed religious principles, zeal, and a ready obedience.

Burning with a noble desire, these early missionaries sacrificed much for their work, and after trials and hardships, for ships were slow and voyages long, reached a land where everything was new, and, for their purposes, crude and amorphous. They found a race just startled from the dream that the arch spanning their horizon was the only world, that they were the only people, and that beyond them and theirs was nothing. This people, plastic for the moulding, saw in the white man, with his superior intelligence, as manifested in material things, a sort of demigod, linked to their island and its gods by scarce remembered traditions, and dimly shadowed in predictions which had come from all time with the softened angles and blurred faces folk-lore acquires in rolling towards us.

What a field it was! And its fruits!

It is always dangerous for a sailor to write of missionaries, for by some queer twist of reasoning he is ranked
by the societies as an enemy to their systems. Yet nothing is more senseless, for of all who drift about the world
no people, as a class, see missionaries and their work more
closely, and more willingly bear testimony to the high
value of the good men, or more persistently keep silent as
to the failings of the indifferent workers. But it should
be set down here that intelligent men long resident in
Polynesia claim that the greatest good resulted from the
stern paternalism of the early missionary rule; while other
men, equally intelligent and experienced, declare that the
only real result, in a religious sense, was to make a fair
number of doubtful Christians out of a nation of really
zealous heathens. And this, too, among a people whose
religion could not have been utterly bad, since its profess-
ors were gentle in nature, brave in battle, moderate in con-
quest, and so utterly separated from the races about them
that cannibalism was unknown. They did, on occasion,
make living sacrifices, notably in seasons of national distress, but no record exists of any sacrifice of the "long
pig," as they euphemize cannibalism. The fact that these
sacrifices no longer exist, that the "Marais" where the religious murders were committed have become the play-
grounds of the children, is quoted as proof of the good that
was done; but then good is always done by the association
of an inferior with a superior order. It is certain that
in many ways the natives were taught to lead better and
purer lives. Chastity was preached and modesty inculcated;
marriage ties were made firmer and divorces more difficult;
and in various directions the heathen mind was turned
from customs more sanctioned by their ignorance and the
example of their forefathers than by the rules of right and
wrong. Sacrifices were abolished, polygamy was forbidden,

and women were raised to a higher place in the domestic
scale. They learned honesty, not that they were thieves
or liars before, but the intermingling of families begot
peculiar ideas of *meum et tuum*, and an airy style of walking off with the goods of others was excused upon the
grounds of possible need and probable consanguinity.
They built better houses, attended to drainage, and gave
up a slavish dependence upon multitudinous gods, not
even fearing to disembowel that great blue shark—son of
this and cousin of that to untold generations—which before they had fed and encouraged with barbaric pomp and
traditional fear. The men and women clothed themselves,
sacrificing grace and æsthetical requirements to Old World
ideas of propriety, though it is to be feared or hoped that
in this the leaven still lingers. The men, in a spasmodic
religious reaction to which such natures are prone, gave up
their loved and medicinal kava, because it was mildly in-
toxicating, and after a time, whether to drown dull care—
for care, like sin, came in with the law—or to ape those
other white men, not missionaries, who drifted to their
shores, took to orange rum, and later to beer and brandy,
and so down the prohibitory scale until they thirsted for
square gin.

With these other adventurers, whether traders or beach-
combers, came new perceptions and a gradual drifting
from the plane upon which their minds had rested. Here
the natives reasoned in a natural though untrained way,
—here were men who did not arrogate to themselves all
the virtues, who followed neither by precept nor practice
a religious life, who liked the free living and the diminished costume of the natives and adopted both, and yet
handled tools more deftly, built better boats, had more of
the worldly goods that really make the Tahitianized heav-
en, and in trade were more liberal and in purchase less

exacting. Jolly good-fellows all were they, and fond,
notably when at flood tide in their cups, of telling the
heathen that while he was of course lower in the scale of
creation than white men, yet the earth was meant for enjoyment and not as a prison where he who goody-goodies
most has the best chance for salvation. This was the
doctrine to suit the very much hymned and more preached
at natives; and with white men to sustain them, the natural consequences were that the missionaries fell from
high Olympus, and for a season the flocks strayed into
bare fields of worldly wickedness. The law was called
in to awaken the slumbering consciences, and while
the severities and restrictions which can be imposed
when politics and dogma go hand in hand frightened
most into a neutral condition, they drove others, generally the high-spirited and more intelligent, into regions
whence no pleadings could ever lure them. Anathemas
were hurled at the offending white men, and at once
all the intolerance against other foreigners and other
creeds which had been smouldering for years and years
burst into a sudden flame that no concessions could
quench or smother.

At a fair average the beach-comber was not a moral
man nor a man of fine perceptions, but he had been lord-
ing it patronizingly over the natives, and did not like
being held up as a personification of all evil—as a Poly-
nesio-Spartan terrible example. In his tipple, which
was often, and out of it, which was seldom, he told many
unpleasant truths. He put into the heads of the natives
wicked, worldly ideas of rights of property, tithes, and
domestic interference; and bellowing that he'd be this'd
and be that'd, after the beach comber manner, if he
would stand it, he bade Jackee strike for his altars and
his fires. Inspired by the alcoholic eloquence of the in-

dignant white man, Jackee did strike, and against everything that he had before accepted in a lazy, unquestioning
mood.   As open rebellion was opposed to his nature, he
often led two kinds of lives: one of public prayer, the
other of private immorality.   With all their acuteness, the
missionaries neither knew this, or, knowing, were powerless to correct it.

After years of bickering the beach-combers and the
Jesuits were expelled; and then, scape-goat for all ills, the
French, with the pomp of military government, usurped
the power of the missionaries.   Forgotten were the enor-
mities of the stranded white men, lost the recollections of
the apostasy of the natives, and if one may believe the
religious societies, the death of everything that had flourished before dates from French possession.   Perhaps a
wise policy would have designated special groups as
the special fields for each sect, for had the integrity of
these territories been maintained, there could have arisen
no clashing of opinions, political or moral.   When all is
said and done, however, the breaking down of the old
barriers at least argued more liberality of spirit and a
more healthful appreciation of the views held in well-
organized communities, and for this the French deserve
praise.   As it was, all the sects founded schools and labored zealously, if bitterly and resentfully, seemingly for-
getting that they were preaching one God and really for
one end.   It is difficult to say which did the most good
or which was the most powerful.   In his wife and in his
home life the Protestant had his most powerful auxil-
iaries, but in the pomp and ceremonies of the Catholic
Church there was much that appealed to the native mind.
The longer residence of the earlier missionary, his greater
wealth, and the fact that he was often Tahitian born,
made the balance at times seem to lean his way; but the

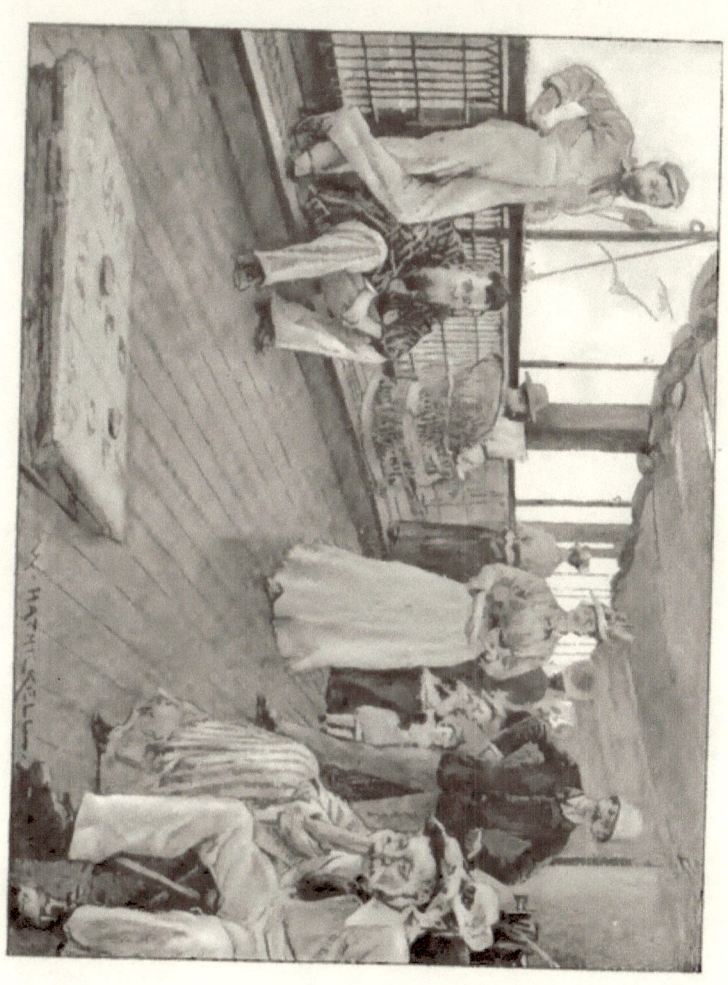

tendency of the government, the close union between Church and State, and, be it said with all fairness, the superior culture, training, and adaptability of the priest, more than compensated for what at first seemed overwhelming advantages.

IV

FAIR-MINDED men were agreed that the severity of the French rule had retarded the prosperity of the islands by dwarfing their industries and crippling their trade. These are, of course, among the normal results of all purely military governments, and are certain to operate wherever the challenge of the sentry replaces the watchman's warning hail. So far as municipal demands went, great improvements were made, for the streets were kept clean and guarded, shopkeepers were held with a tight hand, sanitary regulations were prescribed and obeyed, and citizens and strangers were secured in their life and property. Malcontents insisted that, owing to license and tax, the property so carefully watched was valueless because it finally reverted to the home government, and it is true that taxes were oppressive. The payment of these fell upon the white men; and as the assessments, so often made, had to be satisfied by less than one thousand people, some of whom rejoiced in the immunities of beachcombers and adventurers, the burden was unduly oppressive, whatever its achievements. The government was certainly unpopular, and the fear inspired by the garrison plainly showed how strictly municipal regulations were enforced. Detachments of the marine infantry and a body of gendarmes, assisted by native constables or *mutois*, constituted the police force, the last named doing their duty with a mild sort of protest, as if they hated to spoil sport. When they made an arrest they slunk off with the offender as if they were the real culprits, and their strongest handcuffs were pieces of hemp twine. Regulations concerning women were necessarily strict and were rigidly enforced, especially by that magnificent mystery the gendarme, who was everything ten times multiplied that his brother of Paris loved to be considered. Women were arrested if found upon the streets after gun-fire without passes, or if discovered at any time entering a bar-room. In this case the proprietor was fined cumulatively for the first and second offences, and for a third paid a heavy penalty and had his place closed. Punishments were largely of a practical kind, minor sentences being to work upon the roads and public buildings. The excellent condition of the thoroughfares was due to this; and as drunkenness was a common offence, most of the natives had at some time or another performed this work. Hence no one lost caste by the enforced labor, and the early morning sweepings were apt, Tahitian like, to be more a frolic than a solemn satisfaction of the law. Markets were regularly held, and all buying and selling had to be done in the places established, any speculator caught trying to do a little business on his own account being severely punished. During the protectorate period the power of the queen was always nominal, and it was only upon rare state occasions that she appeared officially to her subjects. She was very popular, and her people realized thoroughly the situation in which fate had placed her. She knew, too, her limitations and their indignities, and there were times when she protested against both; but the "oui-ouis," as the French were contemptuously called, made her realize that the satisfaction of the royal butchers, bakers, and candlestick-makers depended upon her docility. When the ceremonies of her state appearances were at an end, she retired to her residence at Pa-

paoa, and there solaced herself with unlimited euchre and
with the regular visits of her kinsmen, who ruled with
mild pro-consular sway the other islands of the group.

Tahitian society was divided into two classes—cliques—
what you will—and the line of demarcation was as fixed
as the laws of those ancients we are always quoting. One
consisted of whites, pure and simple, and the other of
half-castes. Both were charming, but, oh, so disdainful,
so abusive of the other!—one all dignity and virtue, the
other all mirth and good-nature; the whites horrified if
you associated with the half-castes, and these always delighted to meet you, provided you were neither a prig nor
a snob. Can it be doubted which was more popular with
the nomads? For while wealth, beauty, and education
were equally divided, piety, angularity, and prudishness
were not, and surely there are times when our edifying
virtues become tiresome. The half-castes had delightful
manners, and in their simple gracious conduct there was
nothing of rudeness nor any lack of refinement.

Not much can be told of the domestic life of the
natives, for it is only after years of dwelling among them
that this inner, unwritten life may be understood. If
cleanliness be next to godliness, however, then these
Tahitians may hope confidently for future good. The
clear running streams afforded the most healthful and
delightful bathing-places, and these were used incessantly,
for, contrary to the usually received impressions, the natives
seldom bathed in the open sea or bays. A native woman
with a soiled dress was a rare sight, and so scrupulous
were they in this particular that it became a badge which
distinguished them from the females of the other islands.
Native necessities were few, but these included liquor in
some form. Both sexes were inveterate smokers, the men
indulging with equal gusto in anything from a jack-pipe

to an Upmman, the women contenting themselves with
the dried bark of a native tree. They were hospitable to
a fault, and their cooking would have delighted a Brillat
Savarin ; indeed, when one came to know it well, there were
new delights in the mysteries of their kava. They were
honest, and so willing that it was a new sensation to
employ them, but, withal, paradoxical as it may seem,
lazy in everything that pertained to their own welfare.
Nature had been so bounteous in soil and climate that
there was no need of labor; and as the duties of family
men were narrowed to a *dilettante* sort of fishing, farming,
and fruit-gathering, they had no incentives for gathering
the almighty dollar, nor any opportunities to which they
could devote their energies. From all this resulted the
moral degradation to which in one sense they had fallen ;
for as in the Hawaiian language there was no such word
as virtue, so with the Tahitians there was no appreciation of its meaning. The ancient and unexplained custom
of giving a child at its birth to friends or relatives was
a fruitful cause of this ignorance; for the practice had
weakened those tender relations that should exist between
the parent and child, and through it, doubly, between the
parents. That this universal want of morality existed,
and that it continued despite missionary and lay government, legal enactments, and the example of the white
settlers, proved how deeply it had taken possession of
their otherwise easily guided natures. Like the Tongans,
Hawaiians, and Fijians, the population has steadily de-
creased, the ratio of births not equalling the death-rate,
and it requires no profound ethnological knowledge to
assign the causes.

The Chinese were the money-makers of the island, and
there was a thriving colony of these conservative people,
in no way different from what they were at home or in

that new Cathay, California. Many had intermarried with the natives, and were excellent husbands and citizens, and in assuming their new interests they had opened avenues of trade and gathered hoards of barbaric coin. Can the speculative mind fancy a Chinese colony arising phœnix-like from the ashes of Tahiti?

Upon large plantations, as at Antimaos on the lee-ward side, native "labor" from the Hervey and the Cook groups was employed. This was really a form of slavery, the supply for which, until it was regulated by war-ships, had been controlled by as cruel a set of swashbuckling brutes as ever "black-birded" on any coast or sea. The trade was carried on in smart schooners and brigs, which worked to the southward and westward, picking up cargoes wherever prisoners could be secured from warring chiefs, or, failing that, wherever helpless natives might safely be "run" through trick and device. The wages promised were about $24 yearly; but those paid were actually what the employers chose to add to the little looking-glasses and the stores of beads, cloth, needles, and fish-hooks furnished as enticements to engage. The bounty or head-money demanded by these South Sea "Elizabethans," as jingoes might delight in calling such murderous jail-birds, was always high and exacted upon the spot. It is true something was paid to the chiefs for the slaves supplied, but often there was no one to whom a bonus could be offered, for when peace or other causes closed the usual avenues of slave supply, these pirates anchored inside dis-tant reefs, and luring the natives on board, rushed them below, made sail, gained the open sea, and shaped a course for other groups where the cargo was sold at a fine profit. Once a smart schooner anchored near the entrance to the port of a village which was noted for the kindliness of its people. The captain, skilled in sea deviltries, sent word ashore that a famous missionary would the next day hold religious service on board, with music, and that subsequently he would distribute tracts and Bibles. At the appointed hour the mate dressed himself in canonical garb, the ship's bell was tolled slowly and solemnly, and the natives swarmed on board and below, where the ample, clean-swept holds had been rigged for church. When the 'tween decks were filled, the mate, who knew the native dialect, started the service with a favorite hymn, the accompaniment being played by a pious ship-mate who was famous for the volume and the variety of his " chanties." The natives joined earnestly and melodiously, the mingled chorus drowning the devil's work going on above, for by the time the second hymn was finished sail had been made, the anchors lifted, the hatch covers clapped on tightly, and the schooner was threading her way through the coral channel, bound for a distant labor market with the most profitable cargo of the year.

It was no unusual trick for these " black-birders " to run down canoes at sea, and, after rescuing the crew and passengers, to sell them in islands which were civilized enough to have representatives of foreign governments stationed in their principal port. Some of these consular agents were paid servants of the slave-dealers even after a spasmodic effort had been made by one or two of the Christian nations to regulate the trade. Formalities of law were supposed to be insisted upon, and preparations had to be made by the masters of the schooners to pass the perfunctory tests. One of these was ingenious in its simple barbarity. When, by fair means or foul, a cargo was shipped, and the vessel reached an offing, no food or water was given the natives until they were nearly daft with thirst and hunger. The skipper, bristling with an armory, then appeared and answered the pathetic pleadings of the men, women, and

little children by showing one green cocoa-nut and holding
up one finger, at the same time directing the natives to
imitate his occult pantomime. To each of the sufferers
who lifted a single finger he gave a green cocoa-nut, which
is meat and milk to the Polynesian. It is needless to say
that after one performance the company was perfect. The
next day, under parallel circumstances, two fingers and two
cocoa-nuts were shown, and thus the merry game was re-
hearsed, until a limit of four cocoa-nuts was reached, each
morning four displayed fingers securing four cocoa-nuts.
The day before the vessel arrived in her port was, however,
a banyan day, as sailors have it, and no pleadings could
produce the food. When the natives were landed and
arrayed before the consular office, the agent made a speech
which they did not understand, and demanded, in his finest
official manner, for what period, voluntarily and with full
knowledge, they had agreed to serve. Their late skipper,
standing behind the agent, turned this into their dialect
by asking what they wanted to eat, at the same time showing his food-producing fingers. Very naturally four fingers
were lifted pleadingly by every half-starved man and
woman, and by every hungry little child.

"Do I understand you correctly," exclaimed the consular agent, holding up four fingers, "for four years?"

"For four cocoa-nuts," signalled the unsuspecting natives, who had not engaged for a day, and were very hungry
and thirsty.

"Then four years, be it," replied the smiling function-
ary, "four years as the law provides."

The necessary papers were signed, the proper seals attached, and the natives, with their four cocoa-nuts, were
marched to the plantations. Doubtless the consular agent
declared loudly that everything was most satisfactory, and
that skipper and employer were to be congratulated upon

getting so willing a force for five pounds a head—less, of course (this uttered privately), the customary percentage due for fees and services by both sides.

Think of that, men and women with charity and the love of little children in your hearts! For the four years meant all the years of their lives.

V

IF in the bright morning, the sensuous noon, and the
quiet hours between midnight and dawn the chief attrac-
tion of Papeeté was its tranquil aspect, the early evening
until gun-fire possessed surely a witchery which coursed
like an elixir through the blood, for then the reckless Tahitian world thronged merrily in the Rue de la Petite Po-
logne. All classes ebbed and flooded there, all circles
touched, all save the young lovers, who, with arms clasped
tenderly around each other's necks—after the approved
Tahitian way—wandered along the bosky hedges of the
Purumu Road, or to the beach, where the flashing torches
of the fishermen were reflected in a hundred points of fire.
Men from most of the civilized nations of the world were
swept along this avenue with the jocund throng, making
their finest bows and compliments to the native belles, and
accepting smilingly the cigars which these returned after
they had laughingly stolen a puff or two. Gayly dressed
and crowned like nymphs of old, the women slowly drifted along the roadway, singing, chatting, dancing, and all
with such a noble disregard of the proprieties that one's
moral sense drifted dreamily into approving it because,
though it was not right, it was delightful. The shops
blazed with the glory of lavish oil, the open bars resounded
with the interminable sea songs of the sailors, and soldiers,
mariners, constables, and gendarmes forgot their inherent
antipathies and unbent in profound salutations of mutual
regard. It all made a picture out of a fairy-book, and it

needed only youth and hope and inexperience to read its story aright.

If it chanced to be one of the native dance-nights permitted by municipal rule, *toute Papeeté* crowded the dancing-greens. And what a dance it was! what a spectacle of grace, of unthinking happiness, of joyous abandon! There, perforce, went the morally dazed visitors; for a South Sea "hurra-hurra," or "hoola-hoola," is a tradition, and one would as soon leave Paris with the mysteries of the quadrille unexplored, or Coquimbo or Lima with the Samequacker unvisited, as Tahiti without a first, and an undoubted second, glance at this survival from a prototype that must have existed among the festively inclined Aryans, or among those other forgotten revellers who begot the races of this little sphere. It is a dance found in Mexico and in China, in Algiers and in the wilds of Darien, in Egypt and in the Atacamas; it is found everywhere—probably in Upernavik and Kerguelen Land. As these Tahitian damsels danced, so danced the Nautch girls of India, the Gawazees of Arabia, the Chillenas of the coast—so danced every frolicsome female in the world before the trammels of civilization clogged her challenging feet. Where it was born no one knows; but so danced the forefathers—or foremothers, rather—and so will these Tahitians dance for all their time to come.

And this dance, with a few pathetic songs, is all that is left them out of a past which, as faintly pictured in weird tradition, was glorious with deeds that should have lived forever. The better memories of their race are lost, and their longings for something better than their years now give are dead. Year by year they sink in the scale of humanity, and in the century to come the Tahiti we looked upon will be a meaningless name.

10

THE RIGOR OF THE GAME

THE RIGOR OF THE GAME

"When waves 'gainst rocks and quicksands roar,
  You ne'er hear him repine;
Freezing on Greenland's icy shore,
  Or burning near the line;
But Jack with smiles each danger meets,
  Casts anchor, heaves the log,
Trims all the sails, belays the sheets,
  And drinks his can of grog."—DIBDIN.

I

THIS is the hornpiping, jolly sailor as he appears to most people ashore, and as he likes to be taken. But this is mainly nonsense, except the grog—mere ballad-mongering. There is nowhere a better man than the sailor—man-o'-war or merchant—and equally there is nowhere a greater growler nor a worse repiner than this same Jack. He is often far from a smiling person as, with the poet, he casts anchor, heaves the log, trims the sails, and belays the sheets—duties, by-the-way, of which he does not have the least charge, as he has shipped to pull and haul and not to direct. No one blames him for sticking up bluntly, ship-shape and Bristol fashion, for his rights; but he is led so easily by sea-lawyers with jaw-tackles perpetually unrove that he often does nothing when to leeward of the officers but growl and growl, watch in and watch out. There is no ship like his last ship, no good station since he cruised China-way or up the Straits years ago, and there are no seamen, fore and aft, since he and Commodore John Junk, U.S.N. (dead these fifty years) were laid up in ordinary.

In his Jack Bunsbyan opinion the men who follow the sea in these degenerate days are, to say the least, lob-scousers, canallers, mere stokers or baggage-smashers—moon-minions all; and there has not been a trick at the wheel properly kept, not a nine-pound lead hove clear of the cathead, nor a weather-earing passed smartly, since he was paid off with one thousand dollars (squandered in a week) from the *Ticonderoga* sloop of war some time in the sixties.

The truth is, these sheer hulks forget the past, ignore the present, despair ignorantly of the future, and yarn fearfully. For the life of a sailor in the old days was a sad one, and its sadness is shadowed in his songs.

Sea-going always has been and always will be a career of denial and hardship, but up to the end of the eighteenth century these denials and hardships were cruel and rigorous in the extreme. Curiously enough, sea-writers have understated its horrors; and after making every allowance for the malicious exaggerations of Smollett, who was unfitted for the service he abused, it must be admitted that the life was, in essentials, worse than he described it in *Roderick Random*. Cruises were long and heart-breaking; ships were small, ill-equipped, and rotten; battles, filled with appalling slaughter, were frequent; and as no laws of hygiene were systematically ordered or observed, the navy was devastated by the scourge of scurvy. While ships were engaged for months and months in the unrelieved blockades of ports it was impossible to give the men fresh provisions, pure water, or shore liberty; and when to the alertness of mind demanded by this duty was added the strain imposed physically, is it a wonder that

even the strongest broke down? These conditions existed up to the early part of this century, notably during
the blockade of Brest by Lord St. Vincent, when for a
vexatious period of one hundred and twenty days not a
single ration of fresh grub was served the crews afloat.

The only adopted remedy for scurvy — the accepted
anti-scorbutic—was beer; and as water could not be kept
sweet in casks for any length of time, beer, often of the
vilest character, became at seasons on some stations the
chief beverage of crews. Grog as a part of the ration had
not been served out before the middle of the eighteenth
century, though the Dutch were even then accustomed
to give their crews a nip of Hollands before going into
action. The die-hards of England derisively termed this
"Dutch courage," but unfairly, for no men ever less needed a stimulant to valor than those redoubtable fighters
from the dikes, who in their day swept the Channel with
brooms at the royal mast-heads, and burned the shipping
in the lower reaches of the Thames.

This scurvy, which annually carried off thousands of
English sailormen, was more destructive than villanous
saltpeter and grape-shot; for while it is true that in the
Seven Years' War 1512 seamen and marines were killed,
yet over 133,000 died of disease or were reported missing.
Undoubtedly many of the missing were deserters; but as
the sternest precautions were taken against this offence,
the fact still remains that the deaths from the ship-acquired
diseases—mainly from scurvy—must have been enormous.
Indeed, it was not until the return of Cook from his second voyage that the preventive value of lime-juice was
recognized; and it was only in Rodney's time — mainly
through the great work of Fleet-surgeon Sir Gilbert Blane
—that any intelligent, general attention was given to the
hygienic necessities of ship life.

Though lime-juice had been in use since 1796, Lord St. Vincent was the first to make it (*circa* 1800) an inseparable article of sea diet after the crews had been a certain period afloat. The order prescribed that after a month at sea the daily allowance of each man for the next three weeks was to be one ounce of lime-juice and half an ounce of sugar, mixed in a half-pint bottle. After three weeks it was to be served out every other day until the ship returned to port; and the first lieutenant, master, and surgeon were to inspect its mixing and see that it was taken. Other precautions were adopted. Properly fitted sick-bays were substituted for the sick-berths usually rigged behind screens; ships' store-rooms and wings were rearranged with a view to improved ventilation; and dry-scrubbing with sand and holystones on the lower and orlop decks, instead of the traditional washing, was ordered. Frequent airing of the bedding every week when the weather permitted was enforced; and on September 23, 1800, it was announced that all seamen who wished it must be vaccinated.

These and kindred arrangements were planned so judiciously, and enforced with so much system and regularity, that when the fleet at length returned to Torbay on October 19, 1800, there were only sixteen cases for the hospital out of the 23,000 men who composed the fleet.

After a while—say in the last quarter of the eighteenth century—rum came in as a part of the regular dietary, and the service of its *tot* took up the character of a duly honored ceremony. Everybody drank in those days, from lord high chancellors to fish-wives; and sea-going people, who were especially notable as bottle-men, drank, revelled, and swore fathoms deep and high. And such beverages! The most approved were stingo, bumbo, and hypsy, the last two dreadful compounds of rum, brandy, or wine, all young and fiery, tempered with sweet cordials or disguised in spices, and usually gulped blistering hot. Think of those tipples and their next mornings! or, for that matter, imagine the later revivers of George Osborne's time, when, as Thackeray tells us, the roisterers of the regiment cooled their matutinal heads with small beer.

Sea language was pithy and picturesque, and its oaths were frequent, fierce, quaint, and thunderous, larded with archaic aspirations as to your eyes and limbs, and briny and brimstony in similes. So common was this vice that it was boastingly asserted of Admiral Sir Charles Saunders, "he was never known to swear on board ship"; this abstention *on board ship* being an almost inconceivable mark of self-restraint, worthy of the angels, to whom Admiral Hawke compared his two victorious captains at Quiberon. This mention of a famous sea-fight recalls not only the neglect of the fleet by the government, even after a victory which had saved the Islands from invasion, but the consequent popularity of an epigram written of the "Great Fifty-nine" (as the battle was called), which goes as follows:

> "Ere Hawke did bang
> Monsieur Conflans,
>   You sent us beef and beer;
> Now, Monsieur's beat,
> We've nought to eat,
>   Since you have nought to fear."

The navy was almost entirely recruited by impressment, and this was carried on with unnecessary hardships, often with great cruelty. Bounties were offered for seamen who volunteered—who were "persuaded," as the phrase went —but none was given to landsmen, of whom a good proportion was carried in every ship. When free enlistment failed to secure crews, and it always did fail in war times, recourse was had to the "press." The excitement and rewards of this became a disease almost, for even when persuasion might have succeeded, and a reasonable security existed that enough men would come in, the quicker method of compulsion—pure and simple in its brutality—was adopted.

Press-gangs were recruited from the sailors who habitually enlisted in the navy—the backbone of the service they were fondly called—and these heroes of the doctored dram, the slung-shot, the cudgel, and the deft hanger, were put in charge of "active officers," this being usually but another name — a euphemism — for rum-hardened, determined ruffians of the sword. These gentry established rendezvous in the sailor districts of the seaport towns, and here men were gathered—freely, when they would come, but mainly by clapping hands on them or bludgeoning them. Other active officers were given command of brisk and handy tenders, which swarmed at the mouth of the Channel, awaiting the hapless crews of homeward-bound merchantmen. When the sail was sighted the cutters made a tight race for first entrance, and the ship was brought all standing into the wind by a gunshot across the bow. Occasionally the shot plumped on board, or the ship resisted, and then some of the crew were maimed or killed. A notable case of this kind happened when one of Rodney's lieutenants attempted to board the ship *Britannia* off Portland Bill. In the mêlée which followed resistance four poor fellows were killed by the boarders of the tender *Princess Augusta*, Lieutenant Robert Sax commanding.

The men thus taken out in the king's name were given scant justice, as they were forced to serve any indefinite

BREAKING A RECORD

period on any indefinite station, and often without so much as an hour's sojourn on the land they had sighted after months of deep-water sailing.

The simplicity of this plan made it much favored, as it did not interfere with trade nor arouse the clamor of merchants who had a vote, and it saved the press-gangs a deal of trouble hunting the men in the back streets of towns and along the dusty high-roads. Of course it was a cruel fate for the poor fellows seized in such a brutal fashion just as home lifted above the horizon; but brutality was at a premium then, and the sea ruffian was a "bucko" beloved of the state. Then, too, it was legal enough, a survival of that Crown prerogative by which, for example, Edward III. ordered the Lord Marchers to bring up just as many Welshmen as were needed for his French wars. Its downfall was due to Wilkes—during the Wilkes and Liberty period—but not for poor humanity's sake. He saw in its suppression a political lever, and he pried with it until he toppled over the system and his enemies, despite the frenzied insistence of Chatham, who implored the Ministers to authorize its practice if they wished England to maintain her place among the nations. Indirectly some good things came out of it, for it gave her Captain James Cook, the discoverer, one of the famous sea-worthies of the world. When war broke out between England and France in 1755 a "hot press" was ordered; Cook, then mate of a collier, was lying in the Thames, and, as a prime seaman without particular friends, he was a shining mark for "the persuasions"—the wise call it— of the recruiting officers. He went in hiding at first, but finding his precautions against the crimps and the gangs in vain, he determined to go to Rodney's rendezvous in Wapping and, like the long-headed Yorkshireman he was, secure the bounty and the prospect of advance-

ment as a volunteer, rather than be seized as a pressed
man, for whom there would be neither shillings nor
ratings.

It was the turning-point of his life, and he refers to
it with quaint thankfulness in his journals.

II

ONE thing, however, both volunteers and pressed men were sure of—share and share alike—if they failed of a sharp eye to windward of the officers' favors, and that was flogging. For this punishment was nearly as common then as morning colors, and was so generally ordered that even when the humane Cook came to his command, notably in his First Voyage, the cat was never spared if occasion demanded. We are told in the narrative with grim particularity how it was inflicted upon the butcher of the *Endeavor*, who had threatened to cut the throat of a Tahitian woman with a reaping-hook because she had refused to give him a native stone hatchet in exchange for an iron nail. When the charge was examined and established, orders were given for immediate punishment. The sanguinary butcher was stripped and triced up to the gratings in the rigging, "the Indians preserving a fixed attention and awaiting the event in silent suspense. But as soon as the first stroke was inflicted, such was the humanity of these people, that they interfered with great agitation, and earnestly entreated that the rest of the punishment might be remitted. To this, however, the lieutenant" (Cook's grade at that time) "could not, for various reasons, give his consent, and when the natives found that their intercessions were ineffectual, they manifested their compassion by tears."

I am sure that the lieutenant did quite right, and that the butcher deserved an exemplary dozen, well laid on.

Many of the old shellbacks considered flogging simply
as a disagreeable necessity of their service, and thought
so little of it as a degradation as to have preferred it to
the alternative of stopped or watered grog, or of deprivation of liberty ashore. The truth is, it was made too
common to strike that terror to the soul of the hardened
which would—if anything could—have excused it as a disciplinary measure. I have never heard old officers regret
its abolition, though I have often heard them condemn
its brutality. Still, it was highly valued in some countries, notably in England, where even to this day the
ships' boys may be birched for minor faults, and in rare
cases the older men are flogged for particularly heinous
offences. Even among yachtsmen permission to flog
was asked; notably by the Earl of Yarborough, Commodore of the Royal Yacht Squadron, who offered the
Admiralty a gift of £1000 if he could be accorded the
privilege of tricing up the black-listers of his crew and of
giving them a proper allowance of the cat, which with
his lordship doubtless meant the innumerable dozens of
Dick Deadeye.

In the merchant service as well as in the navy the master enjoyed the right, under sanction of law, to adminis-
ter this punishment, and, what is more, he was expected
to give it in person. But in 1850 the cruel privilege was
forbidden to all ships flying the American flag. Upon
very high authority the law was construed to include the
use of the cat-o'-nine-tails and every similar form of punishment, but not necessarily to mean all corporal punishment, such as a blow with the hand or with a stick or
rope; and in a case cited by Parsons and tried in Boston
it was held that the statute was intended to apply to de-
liberate flogging by way of punishment, and not to a blow
or blows of any kind inflicted in an emergency to produce

immediate obedience. In the navy, however, the third section of the eighth article of war authorizes such punishment as a court-martial may inflict upon any person in the service who quarrels with, strikes or assaults, or uses provoking or reproachful words, gestures, or menaces towards any person in the navy, and, with a full knowledge of its consequences, this very proper provision of law is rarely violated.

Flogging was always an affair of ceremony on board ships of war. On the morning of the day appointed the offenders were brought to the mast by the ship's police, and all hands were piped to witness the punishment. The boatswain's mate, with the cat in hand, stood by the gangway, and near him in due order stood the officer of the deck, the first lieutenant, the captain, and the surgeon. The other officers were ranged on the quarter-deck, and the crew was mustered in the gangway and abaft the mast on the port side. The offence and sentence were read aloud, the culprit was stripped of his shirt, triced up by his hands to a suspended grating, and as the lashes were deftly laid over his bare back a petty officer called out their number. The hardened old tars took it philosophically enough after their first anchorage under the biting thongs; but many a brave lad's spirit was broken by its unpardonable brutality, and many a promising career was shunted into evil by the stinging cross-cuttings of that devil's lash.

Of course tradition lingers over many service yarns spun about scenes at the gangway, but there is room only for that one which describes how a Jackie, ordered to receive his regular half-dozen, thought he might escape it by having a picture of the crucifix tattooed over the whole surface of his back, with the legend pricked around it, "Don't dare strike your Master!" When he was next

stripped at the gangway he turned his India-inked back
to the grim old commodore and said: "Look here, sir,
and read that." "Very good, my lad, very good," re-
sponded the officer; "we will not desecrate the picture.
Mr. Roundshot," turning to the first lieutenant, "have
this man's shirt put on, take off his trousers, lay him over
the breech of a gun, and give him a half-dozen extra.
Oh no! we will respect your scruples, Barnacle; and,
boatswain's-mate, lay the lashes on well and—religiously."
It is said his messmates' ridicule was so great that he deserted the ship at the very next port.

Keelhauling was a method of naval discipline particularly in vogue with the Dutch navy; for as Van Tromp
swept the Channel with a broom at his mast-head, his
countrymen sometimes used human sweepers under their
keels. In large square-rigged vessels the victim, with iron
weights secured to his feet, was lashed to a spar; spans
were carried from this spar to lines which led to the main-
yard. When all was ready the culprit was swayed aloft
to the yard-arm, dropped into the sea, and then hauled
under the ship's bottom from side to side. Here is the
way Marryat describes its performance in the small cut-
ter where Smallbones suffered and Snarleyow was thought
to be a dog-fiend: "This ingenious process," he writes,
"is nothing more nor less than scudding a poor navigator
on a voyage of discovery under the bottom of the vessel,
lowering him down over the bows, and, with the ropes, re-
taining him exactly in his position under the keelson,
while he is drawn aft by a hauling-line until he makes his
appearance at the rudder-chains, generally speaking, quite
out of breath—not at the rapidity of his motion, but because when so long under the water he had expended all
the breath in his body and induced to take salt-water in
lieu. . . . In the days of keelhauling the bottoms of

vessels were not coppered, and in consequence were well
studded with a species of shell-fish called barnacles; and
as these shells were all open-mouthed and with sharp,
cutting points, those who underwent this punishment
(for they were made to hug the keelson of the vessel by
the ropes at each side fastened to their arms) were cut
and scored all over the body as if with so many lancets,
generally coming up bleeding in every part. But this was
considered rather advantageous than otherwise, as the loss
of blood restored the patient if he was not quite drowned,
and the consequence was that one out of three, it is said,
have been known to recover after their submarine excursion."

No words can add to this weird, if somewhat mixed,
description of a very old and hearty sea way of murdering.

Besides these physical miseries, many officers of the
lower grades who were without influence, and most of the
men, whether volunteered, shanghaied, or pressed into the
service, were systematically robbed or defrauded. Indeed,
everybody below command rank was underpaid and defrauded.

Here is a picture painted in 1767 by Captain Augustus
Hervey, when he succeeded in passing through the House
of Commons a measure for improving the half-pay of
naval lieutenants by the addition of a shilling a day to
the miserable pittance of two shillings, which they had
hitherto received: "The lieutenants on half-pay are now
starving for want of subsistence, hiding themselves in the
most remote corners of the country, some for fear of
gaols, which their necessities and their misfortunes, not
their faults, have reduced them to be afraid of; others, to
hide their wants from the world, being ashamed to appear
where they cannot support that character which their
long services, great merits, and a delicate sense of honor

entitle them to. These, sir, in a few years must be lost to the country. Already but too many of them have been obliged to seek with their families a settlement in America. Many are reduced to go as second mates in merchant ships; others have fixed themselves in trades."

The sailor, both naval and merchant, was everywhere the prey of harpies, official and unofficial. For the support of maimed and worn-out naval seamen "a chest" (locked with five keys, to prevent individual peculation) was maintained at Chatham. This fund had been started in the days of Queen Elizabeth by Sir Francis Drake and other sea worthies, and by 1800 had grown, through the accretions of years, into a great sum, capable of relieving many needs; and yet, out of 5205 pensions, only 309 were paid directly to claimants, the rest going to land-sharks who had cajoled the rightful owners out of powers of attorney. Prize-money was also most unequally distributed or withheld, in some cases the shares of the enlisted men being kept by the agents for eight years after the awards had been made.

Merchant seamen were robbed ashore and afloat, but nowhere more scandalously than by the government in its administration of what was known as the Sixpenny Office. Beginning at 1694, all mariners were obliged to contribute sixpence each month out of their wages for the support of Greenwich Hospital, upon a promise that they would be entitled to the benefits of that institution. In 1747 this tax was raised to one shilling, and was continued in its iniquity up to 1851, without the least privilege having been accorded the merchant mariner, whose contributions then exceeded $10,000,000. When the robbery was examined into about 1800, it was learned that the permanent establishment for the collection of the duty consisted of three commissioners: the first, the receiver

of the tax, was an invalid who never went anywhere; the
second, the accountant, was a gentleman of elegant leisure,
who never went to the office; and the third, the treasurer,
was a professor at Cambridge University, who had never
been near enough to the office to know its street or parish.

Even the sick and unfortunate were robbed. An in-
quiry into the Sick and Wounded Office proved that on
board one ship assigned to sick prisoners of war "the surgeon's chief assistant kept a table for the officers at a cost
of £2000 a year, the wretches in the wardroom consuming
the very articles supplied for sick prisoners. The charge
of prisoners of war, when wounded and sick, had thus
fallen into the hands of a set of villains whose consciences
were proof against pity."

In cruising ships matters were, of course, somewhat
better; but the surroundings during nearly the whole of
the sail period were most trying and depressing. In an
article by a living witness—by an officer yet vigorous,
who saw distinguished service, and is an acknowledged authority upon the British service—this description is found:
"A few words," writes Admiral Ryder, "will describe a
sailor's life on board a man-of-war, such as it was in the
memory of many living men. No leave to go on shore
from the day the ship was commissioned until paid off.
No wages until paid off, but occasionally prize-money.
The ship filled with prostitutes in every port by permission of the commanding officer. The majority of the
able and ordinary seamen, and many petty officers, got
drunk on every opportunity—viz., when their boats went
on shore, or by smuggling liquor on board, or by saving
up their daily allowance. Flogging was a weekly, almost
a daily, occurrence. It was almost certain that somebody
would be drunk at evening muster, and punishment was
flogging at 11.30 next forenoon.

"The men, as a rule, could neither read nor write. They were brave as lions, and generous, if utter recklessness with their money when they got it could be called generosity.

"After a three-years commission men had received from £60 to £100 in pay alone, irrespective of prize-money. As a general rule, they lost all their money the first night after the ship was paid off, and the penniless men re-entered for another term of service."

Is it any wonder then that, notwithstanding the punishments inflicted when captured, desertions from such surroundings were so frequent, or that, like Kingsley's "Last Buccaneer," many of them abandoned their lives of privation and misery and turned sea-rover, pirate, smuggler, and sang with him who served under the "Jolly Roger":

"Oh! England is a pleasant place for them that's rich and high,
But England is a cruel place for such poor folks as I;
And such a port for mariners I'll never see again
As the pleasant Isle of Aves beside the Spanish Main.

"There were forty craft in Aves that were both swift and stout,
All furnished well with small-arms and cannon all about;
And a thousand men in Aves made laws so fair and free
To choose their valiant captains and obey them loyally.

"Then we sailed against the Spaniard, with his hoards of plate and gold,
Which he wrung with cruel tortures from Indian folks of old;
Likewise the merchant captains, with hearts as hard as stone,
Who flog men and keelhaul them and starve them to the bone.

"Oh! palms grew high in Aves, and fruits that shone like gold,
And the colibris and parrots they were gorgeous to behold,
And the negro maids to Aves from bondage fast did flee
To welcome gallant sailors a-sweeping in from sea.

"Oh! sweet it was in Aves to hear the landward breeze,
A swing, with good tobacco, in a net between the trees,
With a negro lass to fan you while you listen to the roar
Of the breakers on the reef outside which never touched the
    shore.

"But Scripture saith an ending to all fine things must be,
So the King's ships sailed on Aves, and quite put down were we,
All day we fought like bull-dogs, but they burned the booms at
    night,
And I fled in a piragua sore wounded from the fight.

"Nine days I floated starving, and a negro lass beside,
Till, for all I tried to cheer her, the poor young thing she died.
But as I lay a-gasping a Bristol sail came by,
And brought me home to England, here to beg until I die.

"And now I'm old and going—I'm sure I can't tell where.
One comfort is, this world's so hard I can't be worse off there.
If I might be a sea-dove, I'd fly across the main
To the pleasant Isle of Aves, to look at it once again."

III

In France, then as now, matters were better ordered; but, even at the best, the rights of the sailor were few, and the power of the captain was unbounded. All nations .were supposed to have laws or traditions, though most of these were little honored in the observance, except the one by which some of the Continental maritime nations were perfunctorily governed. This, familiarly known as the Judgments of Oleron, was one of the earliest systems of European maritime law, and is said to have been compiled and promulgated in the Isle of Oleron during the reign of the First Richard.

It was based upon the Rhodian laws and the Consolato, and was so cruel that the great Colbert, moved by its abuses — notably by the one told later — induced Louis XIV. to withdraw it, and to substitute the regulations out of which has grown the present Code Maritime of France. The story set down here of its operation in one notorious instance, taken from Norman's *French Corsairs*, is also interesting, as it throws a side-light upon the character of Jean Bart, of Dunkirk, one of the greatest sailors the world has known. So great, indeed, was this Frenchman that in his day he captured nearly two hundred and fifty vessels of all classes, from feluccas to ships of the line, and once, in 1691, he landed in England and scoured the country in the neighborhood of Newcastle.

In 1666, when sixteen years of age, Jean was appointed mate of the smart brigantine *Cochon Gras,* which was com-

manded by the pilot Valbué. The vessel carried among
its crew a Huguenot sailor, Martin Lanoix, whose religion
made him a butt for the brutal pleasantries of his skipper,
and for the scoffings of all his messmates—save Jean Bart
and Antoine Sauret. This last, a skilled pilot of the time,
and Jean's preceptor, was an old shipmate of his grand-
father and father—one the noted Michel Jacobsen, called
Le Renard de la Mer, and the other Maître Cornil Bart.
Both were famous for their daring and skill among the
Dunkirk and Malouine privateersmen of those valorous
days, and both had chosen Sauret as the teacher of Jean
Bart.

One afternoon Valbué, when more than half-seas over,
spun his open-mouthed crew a yarn of the miraculous aid
offered to a sinking Breton fisher-boat by a ghostly bishop,
who first appeared walking on the water, and then, after
quietly stepping over the side, infused such fresh life and
vigor into the worn-out crew that with more than human
power they stuck to the pumps until the craft was safe in
harbor. When his tale was done, Valbué took the opportunity of launching injurious epithets at his Huguenot
seaman, and of finishing his abuse by hurling a half-empty
drinking-can at Lanoix's head.

With provoking calmness the Huguenot wiped the
dripping cider from his face and beard, and replied, "Master, the Judgments of Oleron lay down that the captain
should be moderate in his language and just in his deal-
ings to his crew—if you please."

Exasperated at the tone of Lanoix's reply, Valbué advanced towards him with uplifted hand and threatening
words. The Huguenot, falling back, continued, in the
same provoking tone, "The Judgments of Oleron, which
bind you as well as me, decree that the captain is not to
punish the sailor until his anger has cooled."

"What!" shouted the enraged Valbué, "you, who blaspheme the Blessed Virgin, dare to quote the law to me! Take that." And lifting a capstan-bar which lay on the open hatch, he aimed a blow at Lanoix's head that, grazing the face, fell full on the sailor's shoulder.

Sauret, as the oldest member of the crew, rose to interpose, but Valbué threatened to strike him also, and the old sea-wolf—as the French grimly call their veterans—knowing the absolute authority of the captain, held his peace wisely.

"Captain," said Lanoix, "I have now received your first blow, as the law enjoins; but now," lightly jumping over the iron rail which ran across the forepart of the ship and marked the quarters of the crew, "now, if you strike me, you exceed your rights, and I can resume mine, for I have passed the chain."

"What!" shrieked Valbué, beside himself with rage. "What! Wait, just wait a moment, and I will show you what laws are applicable to swine, to Jews, and to Huguenots."

Then, seeing Lanoix still on his guard behind the chain, Valbué sprang forward and struck him two violent blows in the face. In an instant the knife of the Huguenot flashed in the air and was buried in the captain's right arm. The gleam of steel was caught by the crew, and, though disgusted at their captain's brutalities, the sense of discipline was strong within them. They rushed to Valbué's aid, and Lanoix was borne down and pinioned in a trice, but not before he had turned on the first man who approached and stabbed him to the heart.

Pale and trembling with fright and anger, Valbué yelped to his mess-boy: "Run to my cabin; there, in a box on the locker, you will find a book bound in white parchment. Bring it to me."

AN OCEAN STEAMER'S GREAT WAVE

The boy disappeared, and in a few moments tumbled on deck with the book in which were set forth the fatal decrees all knew so well.

Jean Bart, taking his trick at the tiller, stood motionless while this tragedy was being enacted. A glance of intelligence passed between him and Sauret, and then the pilot, walking aft, sat on the weather-rail by his youngster's side.

Valbué, turning towards them, shouted: "You know how to read, Sauret; read this."

"I will not read it," replied Sauret.

"Then I will."

"Valbué," interrupted Sauret, "you are not acting according to the law. That unfortunate should be allowed three meals at which he may acknowledge his fault; nay, more: he should be permitted the oaths on bread and on wine and on salt—the three oaths of our judgment—that he may swear to respect your authority in the future."

"Silence!" thundered Valbué. "His blasphemies have deprived him of all right to purge his offence. The chain of refuge, the oaths of excuse, the meals of repentance—these are not for dogs like him. It is not I who judge him, it is the law; I am merely the accuser. Listen! I, Maître Valbué, swear by the Holy Apostles that what I read is the law. Listen, men of Dunkirk!

"'*The sailor who strikes or raises his hand against his captain shall be fastened to the mast by means of a sharp knife, and compelled to withdraw his hand in such a manner that one-half, at least, of the erring hand shall remain affixed to the mast.*'"

Then, half closing the book, Valbué said: "According to the Judgments of Oleron, any sailor blaspheming the

Pope shall have his tongue pierced by a hot iron. Lanoix had so blasphemed our Holy Father, and it was my intention to have carried out the letter of the law for the offence. In attempting to arrest him he drew his knife upon me, his captain, and wounded me in the arm. Now, each man answer in his turn: Did Martin Lanoix blaspheme the name of his Holiness? and, furthermore, did he strike his captain?"

Rolling up the sleeve of his blouse and holding up his arm, Valbué showed a flesh wound, fresh and bleeding. "Answer!" shouted Valbué. "Yes or no?"

The crew, cringing round the captain, murmured "Yes." But from the stern of the ship, in old Sauret's well-known voice, came the words, "Captain, you had passed the chain, and—"

Stamping his foot on the deck, Valbué cried: "That is no answer to my question, son of a dog! Did Martin Lanoix inflict this wound on me or not?"

"But—" interposed Sauret.

"Was it Martin Lanoix—yes or no?" shrieked Valbué.

"Very well—no," said Sauret; and—

"No," echoed the young Jean Bart.

Trembling with rage, Valbué cried: "The law is satisfied. Six of the crew affirm that Martin Lanoix did wound his captain. Two of the crew say he did not. The majority are right. Boy, fetch my cutlass."

The *mousse* dived below, and after a dreadful minute carried on deck a long, straight Spanish sword, that flaunted an edge as keen as a Sikh trooper's *tulwar*.

Stalking forward, Valbué hitched it to the windlass, edge uppermost, and then, ordering the crew to lift Lanoix, he lashed the prisoner's arm to the murderous blade.

"Martin Lanoix, withdraw your arm, as the law directs."

The Huguenot hesitated, and then this Valbué, seizing the helpless prisoner by the throat, dashed him backward; and as he fell, the sword, severing flesh and muscle, laid the quivering arm bare from wrist to elbow.

"Unlash the prisoner."

Faint with loss of blood, Lanoix sank bleeding on the deck.

"Bring aft the body of Simon Larret," was the next command.

"I swear by the Holy Apostles that what I read is true," continued Valbué, again opening the book. "It is the Judgment of Oleron. Listen, men of Dunkirk!

"'*If any sailor kills a messmate, or so wounds him that he dies from the effects of that wound, the living man shall be lashed to the dead and both shall be cast into the sea.*'

"Yes or no—how say you? Did Martin Lanoix kill Simon Larret?"

"Yes," answered the craven six, as before; and—

"No," replied Sauret and Jean Bart—fearless souls both.

"Six recognize the murder, two refuse. The majority are in the right. Let the law be satisfied."

And Martin Lanoix, victim to the hatred of a brutal captain, was lashed, wounded and writhing, to the warm corpse of Larret and cast into the sea of his home port.

But Colbert avenged him.

IV

MARVELLOUS as has been the advance in ships and weapons, still the progress to a higher standard of the man behind the gun, and of his less ornamental brother the man at the main-sheet, has been no less astonishing. To-day the trade of seaman is one worth learning and adopting; for there are prizes for the apt and sober, and a definite prospect of a competency, when self-restraint goes hand in hand with subordinate energy. It is true that in the navy there is little chance, except in war times, for an enlisted man to rise beyond the grade of warrant-officer (boatswain, carpenter, gunner, or sail-maker), or to achieve a commission; but these warrants are very desirable, and are often held by men of the highest character.

As a class, men enrolled in the naval service of any country are finer than the sailors of their native merchant marine, and are surely better treated. In some of the Continental nations advancement and command in the merchant service presuppose an earlier naval enlistment, and the supply for the national ships is sought as far into the heart of the country as the highest spring-tides may reach.

While our system is not so logical, yet we are securing under it many continuous service men, for it is generally accepted that in rations, clothing, privileges, leave, pay, and retiring pension our navy is unequalled in liberality. It has always attracted the best men of the North Atlantic seaboards, and to-day, the world over, merchant-ships of different nationalities are sailed and partly or wholly owned by men who received their training and earned their first savings under our flag. Lately enacted laws prevent all but citizens—native-born or naturalized—serving in our navy; and owing to this, and to the influence of the apprentice system, nearly seventy per cent. of our enlisted men owe allegiance to this country.

This is as it should be, for the navy of the United States is the veritable Fiddlers' Green, the mariner's paradise; and if you do not believe it, ask the first fair-minded, clean-looking, trim-built sailor you meet on the riverfront. He is subjected to discipline, of course, for this is the breath of all maritime nostrils, but in essentials it is neither burdensome nor heart-rending. Disobedience and misconduct are necessarily punished severely, for without subordination and obedience a ship would be imperilled, if not lost. In the old order these matters ran less smoothly and fairly, for there was no specific limit to punishment, and this might be administered in any form or any measure; but to-day the restrictions governing the forecastle control with equal rigor the cabin, and the rights of both classes are defined with a particularity of detail which ought to bar tyranny on one side and mutiny on the other. Between the sailor and his officers there is a community of interests which often works untiringly for the inferior's good, and at times a positive affection exists between the two classes—a genuine respect. No mariner who knows the duties of his station and performs them cheerfully is liable to suffer ill-treatment except under extraordinary circumstances, for it is always to the advantage of officers, governments, and owners that fair dealing should rule the conduct of the ship.

For the protection of ship and crew all maritime countries have codified rules of sea discipline, which with us and the English are known technically as the "Articles for the Government of the Navy," or as " The Articles of War." We derive ours from the older country, and on them rests the foundation upon which the more elaborate codes of the present day have been built. What the "ancient usage" and the "practice of the sea" may have authorized or excused it is hard to say, but the penalties ran the gamut from death to deprivation of liberty to go out of the ship.

At sea, as on shore, hanging was not an extraordinary punishment, and many offences which are now satisfied by imprisonment for brief periods were then deemed capital. In our service a sentence of death may be imposed by a properly constituted court, but since the Mexican War it cannot be carried out until confirmed by the President of the United States. The last execution on shipboard took place in 1847. The culprit was an Englishman, rated as a seaman on board the United States ship *St. Mary's*, at present training-ship in New York, and then engaged in blockading the ports in the vicinity of Vera Cruz. This sailor had been an insubordinate character during the war, and finally reached the culmination of his offences by striking the acting executive officer of the ship, in consequence of a reprimand administered for an infraction of discipline. The general court-martial before which he was tried sentenced him to death, in conformity with the Articles of War, and Commodore Conner, who commanded the squadron, had the punishment inflicted on board the *St. Mary's*. As the unfortunate man was run up to the yard-arm by his own shipmates the crews of all the vessels were mustered on deck to witness the execution. Whether the effect was salutary or not, it resulted in the issue of a general order forbidding thereafter the imposition of the extreme penalty without the consent of the President.

With foreign navies, notably with Russia, the limitations in the matter of capital punishment are not so exact. Indeed, hanging is believed by all English-speaking crews to be so common with the Russians that whenever one of their ships of war goes out of harbor for a day and then returns, our people forward are firmly convinced that the excursion was simply to reach the open sea at sundown, so as to hang a man at a yard-arm clear of territorial limits.

With us general courts-martial alone can examine into the more serious charges, but minor offences may be passed upon by summary courts, while the power of the captain is limited to infractions of the regulations and of the interior routine, his relation, in a disciplinary sense, being much the same as that of a magistrate to a court of record.

No commander of a vessel is allowed to inflict upon a commissioned or warrant officer any other punishment than private reprimand, suspension from duty, arrest, or confinement, and this suspension may not extend beyond ten days, unless a further period be necessary in order to get the offender before a court-martial. Upon enlisted men he may not order at any one time any punishment for a single offence, except one of the following six: withdrawal of any promotions—reduction of any rating, it is called officially—made by himself; confinement, with or without irons (handcuffs), single or double, for a period not exceeding ten days, unless, as in the case of officers, a further confinement is necessary in order to bring the prisoner before a court-martial; solitary confinement on bread and water for a period not exceeding five days; solitary confinement not exceeding seven days; deprivation of liberty on shore; and extra duties. All punishments inflicted must be entered in full upon the ship's log, and the right of appeal exists.

During the civil war our volunteer officers brought into the service many of the disciplinary ideas in vogue with merchant skippers, for there was always a more or less riotous disregard of statute on board the Western ocean packets and the California clippers. Spread-eagling an alleged or genuine offender had, for example, the merit of efficiency, if not of legality. No one, not even when bucked and gagged, as soldiers may tell you, is more thoroughly under control than a person triced up, bat-like, inside the rigging, with hands and feet hauled out to the ratlines of the farthest shrouds, with a loose bight of rope passed round his body, and the head kept from snapping off by efforts at rigidity which prevented protest. For quieting effects it was superior to tricing up a man with his hands ironed behind him and his toes just touching the pitched seam of the deck, inasmuch as an offender in the latter experiment could swear back. Another mode of punishment was to mount an unskilled rider, usually a landsman, upon the spanker-boom, and then, easing off the sheets, to let the wooden horse roll from side to side with the motion of the ship, while the equestrian held on by hugging his steed with all fours or by digging his nails into the wood. Sometimes the motion was so great that the rider was dismounted and broke his leg, or staved in a rib, or dislocated his spine; but as any of these was preferable to a long gallop on the "gray mare," as the boom was called, his legs were usually lashed together under the spar.

Of course all these punishments were illegal, and were the exception on shipboard. Whenever imposed it was done without the sanction of tradition or authority, and wherever reported to the proper officials the officer who inflicted them received summary treatment. For, whatever may be said to the contrary, the discipline of our

ships of war is, in the main, salutary, and its infractions
are dealt with in a legal way.   The conditions surrounding
ship life are so rarely considered by shore people that the
mere mention of statutory punishments is looked upon
with a scandalized horror that would be amusing were it
not so unjust.   More injuries are inflicted in a day by the
police of our large cities than in all the ships of our
service in a year, and these are justified and condoned by
the very people who are most blatant over sea punishments upon the grounds that the clubbed offender deserved it.   The American naval officer yields to no one in
his respect and regard for the genuine sailor.   There are
many such in our navy, there are some in our merchant
marine; but no ship leaves a navy-yard without a definite
number of ill-conditioned ruffians forward who are ripe for
mischief, who make the ship unhappy, and who respond
neither to kind treatment nor to salutary punishment.
No one pretends for a moment to justify any illegal brutality aft, but when these alleged atrocities are examined
dispassionately, with a full knowledge of the environment
and of the circumstances, the employment of the heroic
and effective remedies will be understood, if not approved.

Elaborate as is our code of sea law, too few mandatory
penalties are prescribed by statute.   This often leads to
unfair discriminations, though surely the average deeps
and shallows of a sailor's normal derelictions have been
sounded sufficiently to establish a rigorous rule.   For any
given first offence the imprisonment, irrespective of the
captain's temperament or health or temper, should be ab-
solutely the same for every individual from the beginning
to the end of the cruise.   Jack the favorite should get as
much as Bill the "hellion"; and no punishments, except
in extraordinary cases, should be inflicted until twenty-
four hours have elapsed after the report.

For many years men were at times confined in what was called a "sweat-box"—usually a narrow apartment close to the galley, boarded and sheathed with iron, and perforated with holes for ventilation and light. It was built purposely near the galley, or ship's kitchen, and on a warm day the situation of the occupant was trying indeed. But as some very bad results followed, the department's conscience was stirred, and in March, 1870, a circular was issued by the Secretary of the Navy which declared that "no rooms hitherto called 'sweat-boxes' will be allowed on board any vessel of the navy, but each vessel will have a proper place in which to secure persons sentenced to be confined according to law. No room for this purpose will be smaller than a state-room allowed a ward-room officer in a sloop of war." It is impossible to say how long this means of punishment was used, but it was high time indeed to abolish a torture-chamber where the prisoner would lie stark naked, bathed in perspiration, in a twilight of misery, with lips glued to the holes in the sides of his oven or to the cracks underneath the door.

No tradition tells us by what fiction of the law the youngsters, the reefers, were mast-headed or made to ride the "crojackyard" outside the lifts and braces; or how they advanced in the profession by being sent to "toe a seam" on the lee side in a choice company of greasy mess-servants, lubberly landsmen, and shirking seamen, who had missed their muster, or had gone below when their watch was on deck. How the fond mammas of these suckling Farraguts would have moaned their fate could they have watched their jacketed darlings clinging like grim death to the top-gallant shrouds and swearing their souls away, as they swayed and swung over the angry waters from an airy perch to leeward on the top-mast cross-trees! Why were they sent aloft to buffet the drizzle and the gale?

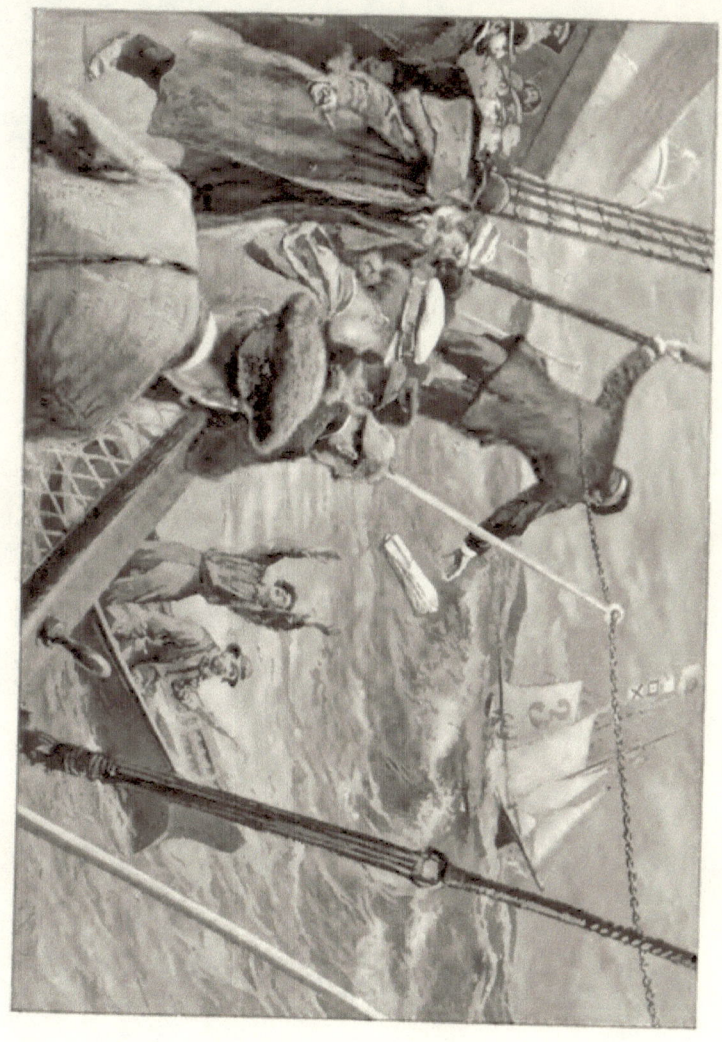

THROWING LETTERS TO THE PILOT

Why was a midshipman ever punished except for two things—for everything and for nothing?

Of course these things are ordered better now, but punishments are still inflicted which are harassing, unnecessary, unfit, and silly. In the old times there was no regulation but the captain's will, no appeal from him, no advancement save through his favorite report. To-day navies suffer from survivals of these traditions; and almost as much as ever does it hold good, certainly in foreign navies, that the lieutenant or junior officer who reports his commander has but a slim chance for the good things of the service. Such an act is looked upon as insubordination, and as the line of demarcation between the cabin and everywhere else is feudal in its character, the subordinate usually has little chance to show anything but the strictly official side of his nature.

And this official side is powerless to explain so many things.

V

IN the parlous days previous to this century, in all services, as in these days with the English and ourselves, the marines were the ships' police, and bitter was the hatred in which they and all other soldiers were held by the old-time mariners. This dislike for soldiers cherished by sailors dated from the early days when the former commanded fleets, for originally the sailors who worked the English ships were not the fighting men. " It was the sagacity of the Tudor sovereigns, Henry VIII. and Elizabeth, which devised a separate class of fighting sea officers trained to the sea. Until, however, the supremacy of the English over the Dutch navy was at last secured, soldier officers and sailors were still much intermixed. It was perhaps partly, besides the natural tendency of things, the rise of such first-rate sailors as Sir John Narborough and Sir Cloudesley Shovel which prevented the recurrence of the old irregularity in this matter. Making their way up from the rank of common seamen, these gallant and accomplished men, trained in the royal navy from their earliest days, proved themselves so perfectly competent for the service in all the requirements of the period that the fashion insensibly changed ; and if a soldier now and then crept in from the court, or from some great family, he found he must relinquish all his former ideas and become a sailor out and out." *

* Burrows.

Still, the scions of good families who were soldiers and not sailors did press their way into a service which was always popular, and by family influence—which was and is still potent in that branch—did force themselves above the head of more deserving men. No one liked this, fore and aft, and the hatred engendered lay at the bottom of much of the discord which wrecked so many joint expeditions. The feeling found expression in the lower ranks by such terms as "land-lubber" on one side, and "drunken swab" on the other; while in the higher grades men like General Mostyn, as reported by Horace Walpole, declared "he was not amphibious enough to like seamen, because there is as much difference between a sailor and a landsman as between a sea horse and a land horse."

All readers of the *Pilot* will remember Coxswain Long Tom Coffin's answer when Captain Burroughcliff tried to persuade him to enlist in his soldier company so that he might secure his life and liberty. "Tom did not laugh aloud," writes Cooper, "for that was a burst of feeling in which he was seldom known to indulge, but every feature of his weather-beaten visage contracted into an expression of bitter, ironical contempt" as he "gave vent to his emotion in these words:

"'A messmate before a shipmate; a shipmate before a stranger; a stranger before a dog; but a dog before a soldier.'"

This was, of course, a briny growl, a rough sea-humor, redolent of tar and marlinespikes, but with enough of shadowy truth to make it palatable to a "fo'c's'le" audience; for those were the days when these hearts of oak endured only their own class, and cherished a curious antipathy to landsmen in general and to soldiers in particular—beggarly lubbers and lobster-backs and jollies, as they dubbed them.

This dislike, up to the second half of this century, included the marines; indeed, its persistency was due to them, for when not drilling and fighting—and there was plenty of both—the routine work of marines on shipboard was police and sentry duty. The proper performance of this brought them into rough-and-ready conflict with all violators of sea discipline; and as the blue-jacket was apt, in and out of season, to run a-muck and to get caught at it, his turn at the gratings came too often to let him feel kindly towards the person who had reported him. This hatred was often encouraged by the officers—at least negatively, and for what they called "the best interests of the service." In some ships the marines were isolated from the seamen by a line as clearly cut as that separating the officers and enlisted men, and any association was discouraged as tending to impair the discipline.

It can be easily imagined that the life of the marines under such circumstances was not a happy one. Their constabulary duties were trying and ungrateful; their charges were enterprising and reckless. Posted between two fires—Coventry forward, black list aft—they got many of the kicks and none of the ha'pence; but be it said that they rarely failed when called upon to assist in the maintenance of discipline and in the suppression of disorder. As both classes progressed in intelligence, and were better cared for in food and pay and in liberty to go ashore, police duties grew lighter; and finally, when hard-drinking was banned fore and aft and the grog ration was abolished, a friendlier feeling was established and the old lines of personal antagonism gradually disappeared.

I say *personal* advisedly, for it must be recognized that the official presence of marines on shipboard is deemed a slur, a reflection upon the seamen, and these naturally ask, "Why should a soldier be hired to watch a sailor?

Why should the billets of sea-going men be taken by people who are not trained for sea work and not expected to perform it?" As it is, the complements of ships are altogether too small for the cleaning, coaling, sailing, and fighting, and why should they be still further reduced by the employment of men who are not sailors, and who do not assist in the cleaning, coaling, or sailing?

These are very interesting and pertinent questions, which somehow seem to fail of an answer.

THE SPIRIT OF LIBOGEN

THE SPIRIT OF LIBOGEN

I

IN one mysterious incident the wreck of the *Rainier* is unparalleled in the history of sea misadventure. Pathetic as are the usual tales of ocean disaster, of peril, suffering, and heroism, this one is individualized by the claimed operation of an occult agency which foretold and to a slight degree aided the final rescue.

The value of the evidence depends, of course, upon the credibility of the witnesses and their object in agreeing upon the same testimony. Of these witnesses one was the chief mate of the ship, another was his wife, the daughter of the *Rainier's* master, and others were seamen of that vessel, who could gain nothing by agreeing to lie persistently in a matter which did not affect their material interests, and who told their common experiences with a frankness and an earnestness no cross-questioning could change.

The indirect evidence rests upon a careful examination made at the time and place by the officers of an American man-of-war. I questioned a number of these officers, and they were agreed that the story was in its essentials confirmed by all the white people rescued on the island of Ujea (pronounced Uji); and that the narrative of the captain and his part of the crew, as described by the Spirit of Libogen, was verified when these mariners were found subsequently at Jaluit, an island of the Rawlic group.

I have followed substantially the lines of the story told by the mate and by the naval officers, giving both such condensation as the differences in the form of the narratives demand. I have no theory to advance as to the unknown forces described, not even the hackneyed one that here—as so often occurs in other stories submitted to the test of psychic investigation—the connecting link is missing or withheld, and that coincidences are mistaken for causes.

II

On the 12th of August, 1883, the American merchant-ship *Rainier*, Bath-built and of 2000 tons' burden, took her departure from the Delaware Capes, bound for the port of Kobe, in Japan. Thirty-five days out the line was crossed, and after a prosperous run the forty-fifth degree of south latitude was reached. Here she was hauled to the eastward for the long run of six thousand miles across the Indian Ocean, on a course that was laid to pass to the south'ard and east'ard of Australia and Micronesia. The average vicissitudes of sea, wind, and weather were supplemented by much sickness and many hardships, but otherwise the voyage did not promise to be a perilous nor an unusual one.

On the 28th of November Norfolk Island, in latitude 29° 0' south, longitude 167° 46' west, was made; and after a supply of fresh provisions had been taken on board, the ship filled away and ran along uneventfully until the tropics were reached. Here the wind failed, and the ship lay idly drifting in that perilous sea at the mercy of unknown currents and uncharted reefs. Many days of fretting calms and baffling airs beset her, but slowly and laboriously the *Rainier* fanned along the course shaped, skirting at a safe distance and at times sighting the treacherous coral outposts of the Caledonian, New Hebrides, and Solomon islands.

On January 3, 1884, the ship then being 144 days out from home, slight puffs of wind whitened the glassy water

with foam-caps, and as the morning advanced these stead-
ied into gentle breezes from the north'ard and east'ard,
gladdening the hearts of all hands with the assurance that
the regions of the brave trades had been reached once
more. As the day grew the breezes freshened, and the
Rainier, listing handsomely under her press of all sail to
sky-sails, slipped eagerly northward—the weight of wind
in her canvas, the clear sky, the unvexed, leeward sweep
of the billows, promising that another fortnight would see
her swinging idly to her anchor in the harbor of Kobe.
About three in the afternoon an island, supposed to be
Lae, of the Marshall group, was raised on the port bow,
and before sundown it bore abeam, distant eight miles as
established by cross-bearings. As this marked the long-
looked-for turning-point in the voyage, the captain changed
the course to northwest, and with a blithe acceptance, for
the ship was clear of the dangerous groups dotting that
roughly surveyed and unbeaconed sea, and nothing was
left save plain sailorizing before the shores of Japan, then
distant about two thousand miles, were lifted.

The moon set near the end of the second dog-watch—
something after 7.30—and a veil of thin mist blotted out
the faint stars as the *Rainier*, sparing her light sails, rushed
into a night that was gloomier than the forecast of the
sundown promised. At eight bells the watch was mustered and relieved, two men were stationed on the to'gallant forecastle, and orders were passed for a brisk and
bright lookout forward. After a careful scrutiny alow and
aloft, the chief mate, who had taken the deck, found the
captain on the starboard quarter, peering with a long
night-glass into the darkness to windward and ahead.
The deck was silent save for the musical noises of a
peaceful sea night, and the decks were steeped in the
witcheries of that pleasant hour, when at last the course

for a long-sought port is set, and the intense watchfulness of days and nights passed in dangerous seas is replaced by a calm alertness which yields nothing in care, but much in wearing anxiety.

The captain swept carefully the open stretches of water, discovering nothing; but as he was about to close the glass he stopped suddenly and focused it earnestly sharp on the bow, and then said hurriedly to his chief officer:

"What is that? There! On the bow—and ahead? Do you see it? A queer white ridge? It looks like white water—it looks—"

"Breakers ahead! Breakers!"

The alert lookouts had seen it, and that dreaded hail, ringing out in the night, penetrated the uttermost living spaces of the ship.

The watch on deck jumped to their feet, the men below tumbled out of their bunks and rushed half-clad to the sheets and braces—every man fore and aft at his station.

"Breakers ahead! On both bows! Breakers—"

The cry rang again and again—there was white water everywhere.

"Hard a'starboard!" sang the captain, and as the wheel swung ardently the port after-braces were let run and the ship's head turned slightly to leeward.

But too late!

The *Rainier* was in the smother of foam, was slipping with a grinding crunching through the outer spurs of coral, and with a dreadful crash, which brought yards and spars tumbling from aloft, struck and stuck on the serrated parapets of a South Sea atoll.

Her day was done.

After a night of dreadful hardship and labor the late dawn broke and revealed a dreary outlook. On both

bows breakers curled and foamed over barriers of coral,
which in some places, notably where the ship had struck,
were submerged, and in others lifted a grayish, crumbling
wall above a turbulent surf. When the day made the
sails of native boats gleamed in the sunshine, and as these
canoes drew near the savages manning them shouted so
madly and with such wild and threatening gesticulations
that death by sea seemed better than the fate which awaited reefward.

It was a desperate situation. The crew and officers
had gathered on the to'gallant forecastle about the captain's daughter, some lashed to the rail, and all hampered
by the tangle of wreckage, though to a degree sheltered
by the quarter-boats, which had been transported forward
during the night. The after-part of the ship was rapidly
disappearing under the incessant pounding of the sea, and
a litter of spars, held alongside by twisted running-gear
and trailing standing-rigging; for these at times darted
like battering-rams against the weakening timbers of the
frames. The sea swept riotously inboard, over the taffrail,
along the decks, through the cabins and deck-houses, up
the steep inclines forward, even into the eyes of the ship
—everywhere—and with such merciless energy that it was
feared the to'gallant forecastle would be carried away, and
with it, in the outgoing current, the hapless company.

The nearly naked savages, ranged knee-deep in the
water on the reef, clamored unceasingly—their king loudest and fiercest of all—and so menacingly that the officers
distributed the rifles and ammunition which had been
brought forward. The morning breeze had not yet freshened, and over the slight space separating ship and reef the
natives shouted a gibberish of mongrel Kanaka, garnished
with the words "captain," "king," "schooner," "whiskey,"
and the like, undoubted inheritances from the white traders

who tramped, half-pirates and half-peddlers, over that sun-
lit sea. Finally it looked as if this blood-thirstiness might,
after all, be due more to excitement than to evil intent, for the king made many pantomimic signs of amity,
shouted "friend," beat his breast, and pointed up the
shining lagoons to two knolls where the island of the atoll
raised its trees shadowily above the horizon.

Reassured by these manifestations, many sea devices
were tried on board to establish communication with the
reef, and so deftly that later the boats were lowered in
a smooth time, and the dangerous passage to the calm
water of the lagoon made with all hands and many
stores. By this time the day was nearly spent, and as
the land, almost undistinguishable from the ship, was fully
ten miles distant, the king determined to sail for home.
The boats were taken in tow, the large mat sails spread
and trimmed, and the convoy sped over the calm water so
speedily that just before sundown the canoes were close to
the beach of an island which was nearly a mile long and a
quarter of a mile wide, and was covered to the water's
edge with groves of cocoa-nut trees. The party landed
after the darkness had fallen, worn to the bone, and wet
and famished, and were assigned to low huts, before which
bonfires of husks were blazing. The shore was lined with
natives, and these by the king's orders brought baskets of
green cocoa-nuts to the half-starved white people. Before
they slept for the night the captain learned that the island
was called Ujea, and that the nearest trading station was
three hundred miles distant. Beyond this he could learn
little, though he tried hard to discover how the natives
knew of the ship's misadventure.

For this was a puzzling matter.

The *Rainier* had gone ashore in the darkness, the natives
had started before daylight, and no lanterns used on board,

13

surely in the mist of that night, could have been seen from
the little island.   Finally the king seemed to understand,
for, lowering his voice, he said, " Libogen speak, Libogen
tell—"

" Libogen?" repeated the captain.

The savage nodded his head, and said:

" Libogen.   Libogen tell—big canoe broke—tell go,"
and then he added, sweeping his hands to encircle the
horizon where the white men might be supposed to live,
" White Kanaka belong Libogen."

III

AFTER a few days given to rest and to recuperation from the bruises and excitement of the wreck, the castaways began to build huts. But nimble-fingered as Jackie is in most things, he was a poor hand at this, and was glad to trade a shirt or a pair of tarry trousers for the three hours' labor by which the deft natives could make a shelter out of cocoa-nut branches and coral grass. The captain, filled with a hundred anxieties, determined to lose no time in seeking a port from which rescue might be sent; and so, when the men were rested, he hauled out the long-boat and made her ready for what, at the fairest chance, would be a dreary and perilous journey. A volunteer crew offered, the boat was soon in as good a condition as circumstances allowed, and on the 10th of January, with the second mate in charge, she sailed before a fresh breeze down the lagoon and into the coral sea.

The captain ordered the mate to hug the wind, and if possible to reach a white man's trading station, called Jaluit, which the natives had said was 300 miles distant. If the wind blew too strong for this turning to windward, the second mate was to run before it to Oulan Island, and if no aid could be found there he was to shape a course for Ascension, and thence to China, which would bear west-southwest by compass, distant 3000 miles.

The weeks following the sailing of the long-boat were bitter with strong winds and rough seas, and cheerless to eyes that waited for sails no breezes lifted above the verge.

Sickness beset them: one man—the steward—died, and others seemed ready to succumb, partly to their miseries and partly to the inroads of the fateful disease which had attacked them on shipboard. The chief mate's wife was in a sad case of physical misery, and the captain, stricken by paralysis, was speechless and almost helpless in his hands and feet. They had no proper food nor clothing; the medicine-chest was nearly exhausted; and their stock of possible presents and barter was rapidly going in exchange for food. The king and his people had lost some of the kindly interest which, in the beginning, the fear of Libogen and the possible appearance of a man-of-war —the *boom-booms*, they called them—had inspired, and, though not threatening, they were sulky.

With the intrepidity of his race and training, the captain determined to build a craft of some sort in which Jaluit might be reached.

"Jaluit," said the king — "*Emid*" (good). "White Kanaka belong Jaluit—plenty, plenty."

On the label of an empty whiskey-bottle, greatly prized by the natives, the captain had seen this name, and reasoned it must be one of the numerous trading stations of the South Seas—one of those sink-holes where, as the pirates infesting it boasted, you could always tell Sunday from the rest of the week because everybody was drunker than usual, and the fights were more frequent and sanguinary.

One day, in hobbling about the island, the captain found a stout timber which the current had stranded on the atoll, and as this was suitable for a keel-piece he set his crew to work. But the king stopped this, on the plea that the old log was too valuable; and finally he had to be bought off by the payment of a large overcoat, which he could not possibly wear, but greatly desired. The work dragged slowly; for though the carpenter was skilful enough, the tools were few and imperfect, and the *Rainier* had broken so fast and so completely that little of value could be secured. Still, the clang of hammer and buzz of saw went on valorously and with such industry that about the middle of March, after fifty-two days of labor, the boat was sparred, rigged, and pronounced ready for departure.

On the 17th of March all hands mustered early to cheer the sailing of the *Ujea*. The schooner was hauled into deep water, and the crew, including Liga Bucho, the king's son, and his servant, who were to act as interpreters in any outlying islands, boarded her. Sail was hoisted, the little anchor was lifted, and with many fervent God-speeds she jumped eagerly into the ripples of the lagoon, took the freshening breeze into her canvas, and soon became a faint speck, and then nothing, in the sky framing the silent waters.

No word came from the *Ujea* for many days; but what happened to her and to the long-boat the hapless ones learned later when the Spirit of Libogen revealed their own and their shipmates' fates.

IV

LIFE on Ujea was dreary enough, and privations and heart-weariness broke the white men's health and destroyed their belief in any hope of rescue. Then, too, the natives began to show signs of hostility; and as there were no longer presents to give, and the strangers were dependent upon the Kanakas for their daily cocoa-nuts and bread-fruit, dissatisfaction ripened into mischief. When three months of hopeless waiting had passed, the mate determined to fit out the two quarter-boats and leave the island. These preparations were watched curiously by the king, and finally the mate confessed his intention. The next evening — Sunday — Noma, one of the king's wives, appeared at the door of the white man's hut with a message from the chief.

In her native dialect and in the Pidgin-English the mate's wife had taught her, Noma explained that Libogen had come to the island and wished to talk with them in the king's house. By this time they had heard much of Libogen, frankly and fully from the king, but stealthily from the others of lower caste, to whom he was *tabu*. Piecing together the fragments of explanation, they gathered that Libogen was a human being who had lived in Ujea, had died in the hut they occupied, and was now buried alone on a little island twenty miles or more down the lagoon, which none but the king and his kinsmen dared visit. Whether Libogen was man, woman, or child, no one could tell; but he was the guiding spirit of the island, the ruler of all who journey by water, the special protector of white sailors, and the adviser of the king, whom it visited at times, and with whom alone it would converse. Speaking at more length of the day of the wreck, Noma had repeated on several occasions, "So, long time gone, Libogen speak king one night. King take canoe, go down reef, find too big canoe, all broke. Plenty white Kanakas. Spose king no good to white Kanakas. Bumby man-of-war come and *boom-boom* king. So he go down reef one morning before sun and see too big canoe all broke. He get white Kanakas. So white Kanakas belong Libogen."

When the mate and his wife arrived at the house the king was seated in the centre of the room surrounded by his family; near the door the third officer and the seven remaining sailors of the *Rainier* were clustered, all listening intently to a mysterious voice which could be heard hissingly, first on one side, next on another, then overhead, and at times in the centre of the enclosure. The king motioned the visitors to a seat beside him, but beyond this no notice was taken of their appearance by the intent groups eagerly listening to the mystical messages.

The room was dimly lighted, and the grewsome silence was broken only by the murmuring of the night breeze through the pandanus-trees, by the muffled echoes of the sea thundering on the barriers up the wind miles away, and by the voice.

This voice was low and distinct, with a curious sibilant quality, and as it ebbed and flowed about the room the mate and his wife, even with their slight knowledge, clearly made out the meaning of many words.

Presently the king lifted his hand, palm outward, and said, "Libogen speak to mate."

After pausing a moment and, as he confessed, very much awed—even granting it was all a clumsy trick of

some native medicine-man—the mate asked Libogen to tell
him three things: " First, what had become of the second
mate and the long-boat? Secondly, what was the fate of
the captain and the thirteen of the crew who had sailed on
the schooner? Thirdly, if he and the others with him
were to be rescued from the island?"

The king slowly asked the questions, and as the faint
whispered replies came, now from here, now from there, at
times even in the ear of the mate, he translated them in
a mixture of dialects which, put together, made this message:

" *The second mate had been picked up by a ship near
an island called Pornipette.*"

Where Pornipette was neither the king nor any of the
white men knew when subsequently this question was discussed.

" *The captain had arrived at Jaluit, was there then, but
too ill to leave ; no trading schooners were in the port, though
as soon as one arrived it would be sent to their rescue. In
one week a schooner would come to Ujea.   In two weeks a
big schooner would come with the second mate, and they would
all be taken away.*"

The voice ceased for a moment, and then followed another message announcing that the spirit of Silva, the steward who had died on the island, was present with Libogen.

Presently the king stated that Libogen had finished, and
told the mate to say " Good-night, Libogen." " Which,"
said the mate, " I did, and was answered by ' Good-night,
mate,' in as plain English as I could speak myself. My wife
was asked to do the same, and was as plainly answered
' Good-night, Emma '—this in the hearing of all."

As the long week drew to an end the king drifted to
the mate's hut one evening to get his usual pipe of oakum,

for the tobacco, and nearly all the tea, had been used long ago. After smoking a few moments he said, "Libogen speak, to-morrow—one week up—schooner come."

"Libogen," replied the mate, nervously, "Libogen tells lies. Libogen does not speak true."

"No, no, no," answered the king, earnestly, "to-morrow come, sun finish, schooner come. Libogen no lie, always speak true."

All Sunday the ten white people watched the sea eagerly from the lookout, where they had raised a flag-staff and laid a fire for lighting. The day dragged slowly, and as the sun declined the hope they had cherished in spite of all reasoning was about to fade, when, just before sundown, they heard a shout go up and saw a confused mass of yelling natives running to the southern edge of the island. The king, who was standing next to the mate, shouted, "Schooner come! Libogen no lie."

The mate brought his sea-glasses to bear in the direction indicated, and made out a curiously built craft, carrying a large three-cornered sail. Many natives swarmed about her decks, and as he watched he feared that the deliverance promised might be from life, but not from bondage. The king, who saw his alarm, said, "Never mind, Kanakas no hurt mate. See? Not come here, go another island."

It was as the king said, for just as the sun dipped the sheets of the craft were lifted, and she rounded the outer points of the atoll and sailed into the mysteries and silences of the ocean night.

It was a queer realization of the first part of Libogen's prophecy, and in their eagerness to find if the coming week should have its fulfilment the days crept slothfully. Even the sky and wind and sea were against them, for it was the change of the monsoon, and the fine, brisk weather

had given way to fierce heat, which was succeeded by tor-
rents of rain and a wearying sultriness that would have
sapped all interest out of life were it not for the intensity
of hope that made the blood run fervidly in their veins.

On Saturday night the mate and his wife sat in their
hut, nervously discussing what the next day would bring
them, both hopeful for the other's sake, when suddenly
she started to her feet, exclaiming, "Listen, I hear a gun
—a loud gun, not the surf—but a gun," and at that moment a native rushed to the hut, crying, "Schooner come
—*boom-boom—boom-boom!* Schooner come!"

The morning dawned with drizzle, and a wet, salt mist
shrouded the land and sea; even the nearest reef could
not be seen, and in the dulled sky no gleam of silvered
cloud showed where the sun was climbing. The crew had
been stationed so that the ocean could be swept in every
quarter, and the officers were about to visit these lookouts
when solemnly and sullenly the resounding clamor of a
heavy gun rolled over the dreary water. As they ran for
the highest point of the island another gun boomed mournfully, and then the mist lifted its heavy vapors, and, borne
crazily on the light airs just making, came from lookout to
lookout that hail of hails, "Sail ho! sail ho!"

Groups of natives stood around the coral-grass on the
knolls, pointing and shrieking wildly; the lookouts danced
and waved their nerveless arms excitedly; the king and
the mate paused in a little clear space—all gazing through
the sphering, sodden haze at a large vessel standing slowly
under fore-and-aft sail and skimming the southwest edges
of the reef.

"Mate, look!" said the king, proudly. "*Boom-boom—*
Libogen no lie. Tell two weeks big schooner come.
Mate, look!"

No time for laggards then, and a rush was made by the

white men for their boat, to intercept the vessel. She might have seen the island indistinctly or not at all; the fog might shut down; a thousand fears and contingencies seized them, and all supreme effort was better than the death of the hope now blazing riotously through their blood.

It was a long pull, and a hot one, and they were weak with illness and want of food, but it was a pull for life and home. As soon as a safe place was discovered amidst the breakers the boat was headed for the reef, dragged on the coral wall, and there held poised until the smooth time came. And when it came, with a loud cheer the craft was shoved into the breathing space of the surf, and with nerved grip and eager heart pulled clear of the breakers seaward.

The fog blew down the wind in pale, hurrying sheets, tinted with glints of the clearing day, and as the sun burst through the upper sky it lighted on the black hull of a war steamer, over which streamed, in the moist, golden light, the folds of the American ensign. The ship was headed towards them, and as they drew under her lee they saw their second mate leaning over the bulwarks shouting a joyous welcome.

It was the American sloop of war *Essex*, sent by the admiral of the China station to rescue the *Rainier's* crew.

V

WHEN the threads of the ravelled yarns were gathered the castaways learned that the second mate's boat had been picked up near the island of Pornipette by the British bark *Catalina*, bound from Australia to Saigon, Cochin China; and that he had been sent to Hong-Kong, where, on learning his story, the American admiral had ordered Commander A. H. McCormick, commanding the *Essex*, steam sloop of war, to the rescue. Two days after sailing from Ujea the *Essex* arrived at Jaluit and the captain and his part of the crew found. What is more, when the captain's story was told, the circumstances of his illness, of the absence of schooners, and of his efforts to send relief were as Libogen had revealed them.

These are the facts in the case, and it is a queer mystery of the sea, an odd but true yarn—is it not?

QUEER PETS OF SAILOR JACK

QUEER PETS OF SAILOR JACK

WITHOUT his breathing-spaces and his play-time naval
Jack would be the dullest of all dull boys. At the best,
sea life is so filled with perils, self-denials, and hardships,
that if it were unlightened the strongest and best would
bend under its strain. Even on the tautest ships this is
recognized, and always the routine of work, watches, and
drills is interrupted by recesses the sailor may call his
own. In these seasons of rest he gets his share of such
maritime pleasure as time and tide may dole; then he
may weave and twist the undisputed yarn in the lee gangway to an audience that never tires nor dares to doubt;
then may he pull placidly at the unvexed pipe, loaded to
the muzzle with the strongest tobacco in the world; then
may he swing dolorously into the dreary variety-hall dit-
ties, which haplessly have sunk fathoms deep the dear old
sea - songs; or, if wind and weather permit, he may bake
on the "fo'c's'le" in the sunlight, and overhaul with minute care his clothes-bag and his ditty-box.

As a rule, the modern man-o'-war's man takes his pleasure seriously, soberly, and in discreet company; for, like
great Pan, the tar of fiction and of song is dead. You
will see him no more fresh from the Spanish Main, garbed
quaintly, and striking the attitudes of a master of dance
and combat; no more will you mark him shifting quids,

hitching trousers, damning eyes, and scattering double handfuls of doubloons and moidores; no more will you see him cross-gartered and pigtailed, sword-girded and bepistoled, save in that weird melodrama where the gods still love him. He is alert, vigorous, self-reliant, frank, modest, brave, temperate. The type figuring in the popular mind as a *die-hard* is the exception; and be sure that the shore rovers, carrying lee gunwales under with a press of canvas, and backing and filling — filling especially — along the hospitable channel-ways of the Bowery, are not true representatives of our Yankee tars.

Week after week I have seen the watches of a ship of war go ashore with the utmost regularity, and return clean and sober, usually before their liberty had expired and rarely over time. I believe no class of similar station is superior to sailor men; and if you doubt this, take a Jackie's Saturday night ashore, and ask the policemen along the Bowery, or search the police records, and the inquiries must convince you. Of course he is not a saint; and while there is no such regular spree as the blue Monday of other working-men, occasional lapses are natural enough. Often, when a blue-jacket strikes the beach, he has so many lost opportunities of conviviality to make up, and land-keeping people are so apt to view him with a regard and a forgiveness yielded no other class, that his good resolutions scurry whistling down the wind, and his normal qualities are eclipsed by the gayeties of the run ashore.

The naval seaman of our day has to think as well as to pull and haul, and he must keep a sharp lookout to windward if he desires advancement in a trade where the specialties are many and the rewards are great for aptitude and good behavior. Then, too, he has been advanced to a higher plane, for he lives better, and is better clothed

and housed, than in the days of carronades and stunsails.
Save in exceptional voyages to distant stations, he is more
often, if not so long, in port, and he has greater opportunities for shore-going—more liberty, as he calls it—and
more systematic discipline. To see him at his best is in
the open, in an emergency calling for brain and brawn,
and next, perhaps, in a port drill, when a rival ship is
pressing hard in a hot race against time. Then will be
revealed a type of honest, hard-working, patient yet eager
manhood that is an honor to the calling and the country.

Jack's life is set about with metes and bounds, as the
requirements of modern war machines may leave uncon-
sidered but few half-hours of the day. Usually he is
called at sunrise, and from then until four in the afternoon he is busy with the persistency of a mechanic, and
alert with the readiness of a doctor for an unexpected
duty. During meal hours he is allowed to smoke within
his prescribed limits ; and so jealously are these times of
rest guarded that a red pennant flying aloft shows to the
outside world he may not be disturbed, even were it to
receive the admiral. After supper there are minor details
to be finished, a routine drill perhaps, at sea often a gun
exercise, but always when hammocks are piped down and
until tattoo is done the cherished leisure hours are made
as much his own as the cares of the ship permit.

This is his season of merriment, and his pleasure runs
the gamut of many physical bouts. He boxes, and gives
play with single-stick and quarter-staff, both vigorous, determined, and honestly punctuated with resounding whacks
and grinning acceptances of pain. The bear is chased
amid much license of noise, and Jack swims, dives, rows,
wrestles, and dances. And how he dances! Save on
board flag-ships, bands are extemporized affairs, for the
sailor loves his music dearly, even when he has to pay his

14

piper, and is a prentice hand with various instruments, though I think there is an unwritten law against the wheezy and soul-envenoming concertina and a respected prejudice concerning the piccolo.

I do not know that he hornpipes it so much as he jigs it; but when he does go in for form and style his traditional performance is filled with strength and grace and honest delight.

It is at this hour, too, that the dumb pets of the crew have their rarest frolic, for by the association, by the inspiration, perhaps, of the same sentiment, this twilight season becomes to the sailor what the children's hour is to the luckier landsman in homes where love is sanctified by the tender witcheries of happy childhood. The isolation of the sailor, the craving during long years of exile for something that cares for him purely for himself, is a charm to conjure with, and lucky indeed is the dumb brute whose lines fall in the pleasant places of the forecastle. Indeed, the fondness sailors show for their pets is proverbial, and so intimately are these associated with certain famous deeds of the sea that they have acquired a definite name and fame, and are as well known and as fondly remembered and lamented as are the racers of by-gone days by ancient jocks and stable-boys.

With sailors this feeling often borders on a sincere affection, and in the early twilight of a second dog-watch I have seen weather-beaten, battle-scarred blue-jackets fondling some pet as tenderly as a mother would her first-born, and then, when darkness fell, stowing it in a secure bed and bidding it the most affectionate good-night. These pets are of every description, from field-mice to bears, at times more than one sharing the allegiance of an owner. I recall an aged foremast-man of one of our sloops of war—the *Vandalia*, I think—who had collected a most interesting family, consisting of a dog, goat, cat, rabbit, hen, parrot, and monkey, all living in a harmony which put to shame the immoral and quarrelsome members of like households in stuffy museums. So well behaved and decorous were they that even the strictest of first lieutenants, watchful for holystoned decks and shining paint-work, could not complain. Another of our war-ships mustered a pig, a bear, and a dog in its books. These had become thoroughly sailorized, going at drum-beat to quarters, mustering with their divisions, and observing with a fine precision the routine of the day. By an unexplained but accepted assumption of rank the pig took his station on the quarter-deck, the bear mustered amidships, and the dog clung to the eyes of the ship, each in the wake of his adopted gun's crew. Nothing was allowed to disturb this ceremonial precedence, not even the riot and roar and the slaughter, when the ship was sometimes hot in the hell of action. At times the bear, with misty recollections of pine woods and underbrush, would cut adrift from the restraints of education and run "amook" in the gangways, more or less violently hugging members of the crew. He showed a fine discrimination between friend and foe, cherishing for days the remembrance of an affront, and never losing an opportunity of avenging it, as many a madcap youngster had occasion to remember.

Of all pets none is better suited for ship life than the wily goat, and the traditions of the navy are jocund with quaint stories of this animal. Once in the good old days of tarpaulin hats and true-lovers' knots a famous ship's company owned one that fell into evil ways, such as chewing tobacco, drinking grog, and challenging the best men in the ship to butting matches. Indeed, he became a very rakish, swash-buckling, eye-damning, timber-shivering goat, who lived long and not well, and died after a prolonged debauch in a fit akin to what Jackie calls " the horrors."

Each day, by common consent, the men added a pint of water to the grog-tub, and regularly in his turn Bill came for his tot. At seasons, when the master's mate of the spirit-room was disguised with overmuch drink, the goat, like his two-legged messmates, doubled on the tub, and secured a smuggled ration. He came to grief at last, for on an occasion when the grog was stiff to his liking he got well to wind'ard of the tub, charged, like a first boarder, over a clear hammock-rail at the mate and purser's clerk, took possession of the marine bar, and got so gloriously fuddled, so gloriously " uncou'fou," that he never recovered, but went overboard in a middle watch through sheer despair and misery.

Another goat was the prized shipmate of one of our vessels wrecked on the coast of India, fortunately in weather moderate enough to launch the boats and rafts. Each man was detailed for his place, and allowed to carry his bag of clothes or his hammock, no greater provision being needed, as the shore was close aboard. As the men slowly lowered themselves over the ship's side, the nanny-goat stood amongst the waiting ones, watching her master, the ship's cook, who stood irresolutely at the mast until his turn came. The cook was an old sailor, and his kit was very valuable to him — it was probably all he had in the world—but when his name was called he dropped the bag, touched his forelock, and said:

" If you please, sir, I can't bear to leave Nanny behind. I'll take her instead of the bag, for there isn't room for both ;" and then, appealingly, " Can I, sir ?"

Nanny went over the side and landed with him, marched by him through the desert, and when relief came bleated her enjoyment in a way that repaid him for the

"'I CANNOT BEAR TO LEAVE NANNY BEHIND'"

sacrifice. For many years she browsed among the scrap-heaps and rare grass-plots of the Brooklyn Navy-yard, where, surrounded by a numerous progeny, she doubtless told, with many butts, the yarn of the day when her cook and master saved her up Mozambique way.

I remember some pets of my sea-going days, cherished in life and mourned in death. One was a scraggy hen, of no known breed, raised in Polynesia, and given to one of our officers by a native woman in Nukahiva. Her abnormal thinness saved her from the steward's knife in the early days at sea; but finally all hopes of fattening her failed, and she was doomed for a ward-room ragout. One of the men, a queer character in his way, who had made a study of chickens, begged permission to keep her, and as we had fresh grub enough, Nell, as he called her, was saved. In a little while it was more damning than a Grain Coast fetich or an Hawaiian taboo to harm her, and Nell thrived and flourished.

She was carried through all the islands down to New Zealand and Australia, and back to Chili and Peru, improving daily, and displaying an intelligence that was surprising. She was the queen regnant of the coop when she deigned to enter, and was as jealous of her prerogatives as the King of Yvetot. Her cackle proclaimed the late tropical daylight before her liege lord for the time being had hailed the morn, and there was a row if Jemmy Ducks, guardian and feeder of sea-poultry from time immemorial, did not hobble aft to give her a morning strut to leeward. The first of the corn and water was hers, and having the coign of vantage beyond the coop bars, all lesser chickens, save the favored chanticleer of her affections, suffered.

She displayed a passion for bananas and yams, had strongly marked likes and dislikes, and, though coquet-

tish, manifested an affection that was not hampered by
official rank, but ran by a descending scale of years—a
white-haired quartermaster possessing more than a tender spot in her capacious heart, while the ship's boys were
held in a contempt beyond expression. The men swore
by all the pet warrantees of their profession that she
whistled and talked, and I know she was as good a storm-
glass as any standard instrument on shipboard. Her favorite roost was over the wardroom skylight, her chosen
time the dinner-hour, and there she would perch, eying,
with respectful familiarity, the senior lieutenant. Her interest gradually increased as the dessert stage approached,
the appearance of the fruit awaking a cooing, beseech-
ing cackle that invariably brought her the ripest banana
or the juiciest mango. She often kept the deck officer
company in the middle watches, dozing to leeward of the
mast until the bell struck, when she would straighten
with an assertive air, as if she had never slept, and cackle
a warning hail to the lookout. Poor Nell died during the
Darien survey, from indigestion and old age, and when
she was carried ashore for burial in the neat coffin Chips,
the Scotch carpenter's mate, had fashioned, we felt that
she had made a place in our lives and memories that some
day deserved its record.

A ship-rat is usually not a cherished object of affection.
but I knew of one, and here is the outline of its story:
Once in the quarterly overhauling of a frigate's main-hold
a rat but a few days old was the only inmate found of a
predatory colony which had scurried off, been captured, or
carried away when the invaders entered. The ship's doctor, a tender soul, took nest and all to his room, rigged
a crude but adequate feeding arrangement, and nursed
and strengthened the baby rat into a healthy childhood.
Nothing could have been tamer than the little gray creat-

ure, and it thrived lustily. It slept in the doctor's room, but made rambling adventures through the civilized plains of the ship, fearsomely avoiding the wilderness and deserts closed to man in the frames and timbers of the hull. At night it always awoke when the doctor came on shipboard, waited for a little food and fondling, and then slept peacefully until reveille sent it scampering to the steward for breakfast. It kept the doctor's quarters clear of all winged insects, and made such a riot among the ants and roaches of the wardroom that the executive officer and mess caterer numbered it among their most efficient aids. It is unnecessary to say that no cats were allowed aft, and that the license and liberties of the officers' quarters were the cherished pleasure and hunting preserves of the rodent. Its affection for the doctor was unbounded, and it shared a particular fondness for the photographs of his children, peering through the glass at their innocent faces, and making a vantage-ground for its mid-day naps upon one of the largest of the frames which hung against the after bulkhead of the officers' bunk.

One night after a shore-going in a tropical port the doctor lighted a candle at the wardroom lantern, and, entering his room, heard a whirring note of anger over his bed. Looking up he saw the little rat in a strange state of fury, its eyes burning like points of fire, its hair ruffled, and its legs gathered for a jump. Wondering at this unwonted excitement, the doctor called and whistled to it, and then turned to his bunk to throw back the bedclothes.

Just as his hand reached the upper covering he heard a strident shriek of anger and the whir of a flying body, and saw, just beneath his uplifted hand, the rat struggling in the bed with an animated ball of fuzzy black that bristled with claw-like tentacles, writhing convulsively. The struggle was sudden, sharp, short, and when it was over the doctor found lying dead on the bed one of the most savage and venomous scorpions of that region.

It had come on board probably in the unbarked fire-wood, and had worked its way aft through the hidden recesses of the timbers to the doctor's room. Had his hand ever touched the sheet where the scorpion rested, hidden from him in the half-light, but visible to the rat, no power could have saved him from the poison of the sting which would have followed.

Of course his ratship was the hero of that day and of many days, and I should like to add that it went on in the pleasant lines of its youth, adding to its virtues hourly. But one night when it had become big and strong it strayed into the evil company of other rats, and crept with them upon strange and parlous adventures. Gradually it forsook its civilization and life of simple honesty, and during a mid-watch close after four bells it was found dead— a prey to a jealous ship-cat who caught it stealing warily towards a mess cheese forgotten in the 'tween-decks forward.

Next in importance, but not chronologically, was a wonderful pig—not a euchre-playing, time-telling, disreputable suckling—but as plucky a four-legged shoat as ever thirsted for a miry spot or ran straw-mouthed in windy weather. What memories clustered around that animated suckling! What regrets filled our souls in after-days for his early flight!

By some lost correlation of ideas pigs who go down to the sea are always dubbed "Dennis," and it is only a little less than mutiny to name them otherwise. This Dennis, I regret to say, was smuggled aboard secretly just as we were leaving Talcahuano, in southern Chili. The truth is, he had been stolen from the bosom of a family of six by our unconscionable rogue of a wardroom steward, who afterwards repeated the performance on shipboard with distinguished success, except in this final scene our money and not the pig dramatically disappeared.

Dennis was discovered by his grunted protests against confinement shortly after we were under way—probably off Quiriquina Island, and too late to make restitution—and his beauty and developing intelligence so appealed to us that he was saved from a growling butcher to become an important member of our ship family. He was entered upon the cook's roster as Dennis O'Quiriquina, which was softened to O'Quiri, and then, in compliment to the land where his race is most prized, into Dennis O'Kerry—as Milesian a title as Brian Boru of Clontarf and all the sons of Heremon could have desired.

It must have been some time in March that he joined us, for I remember on St. Patrick's Day, when the hills back of Valparaiso were echoing with the strains of "Garryowen" and "The Connaughtman's Rambles," played by the flag-ship's band, Dennis trotted aft at merry speed, decked with green ribbons, and carrying a dhudeen around his neck and the mealiest potato in the locker spliced to his corkscrew tail. He appreciated the dignity of the time and place, for when we went to quarters he made a polite bow to the captain, and for the first time in his life asserted and gained his right to the quarter-deck. On occasions of special ceremony he had to be driven forward with contumely, but ordinarily he could never be rooted from the spot, for with the drum-beat he came aft on a run to quarters—blow high or blow low, fair weather or foul—and assumed, to a mathematical nicety, the station selected on the saint's day.

He had his bath at daylight, and was washed and brushed and combed into a state of snowy whiteness which pro-

claimed the possibilities of piggy cleanliness, and then he
feasted in dignified ease within the honored and exclusive
precincts of the galley. During the day he lolled about the
decks, generally in the wake of the spare booms, filled with
the pride of placeship and never awed from the career of
his humor. He attended drills with praiseworthy punctu-
ality, and was in nobody's watch and everybody's mess,
which is the perfect flower of sea luxury. When night
came, in his early days of leanness, he sought his hammock, and, later, his carefully prepared division-tub; but
after a time, when fatness clung to his bones and no sail-
or's bed-devices would hold him, he would airily promenade the deck, waking up a sailor here and there until he
found a shipmate fit for his high nobility. I have frequently seen a man awake in the middle of the night, and,
calling Dennis, give him half his blanket or pea-jacket,
and then, with a contented grunt, Dennis would nestle
snugly in his new bed, and sailor and pig slept the sleep
of the just, their mingled snores filling the still hours of
the middle watch with touching tales of boon compan-
ionship.

But an end came to all this happy time, for Dennis acquired undue fat, and fell into moralizing, sedate, and dignified ways; next he lost his sense of humor, his fondness
for fun; and then, last scene of all, he forgot the laboriously taught proprieties of ship etiquette and sea life.
Could he have been dreaming of the lost wallowings of
his race, the prizes of unalloyed wealth that lay in sun-
bathed mires? The truth is, Dennis degenerated with
his prosperity, and became touchy and captious. We
would have borne with his ailments, for he had sailed
thousands of miles with us, in good weather and bad; he
had been in his day the most dandy and rakish of pigs,
and had such a way of cocking his weather eye knowingly

"'I'D AS SOON EAT MY BROTHER AS THAT PIG'"

to the wind'ard, such a rolling gait, and such an heroic
fondness for 'baccy and lobscouse, that we would have
cherished him to the end.

It was somewhere about the last of June, and we were
at anchor off Papeete, in Tahiti, when the captain said to
me, in his quiet way: "You will have to send the pig
ashore; the executive officer reports him unfit for duty."

Of course, this sealed the fate of Dennis; so I sent for
the man who looked out for him, and said: "Barbe, my
lad, it will be the Fourth of July next week, and Dennis
has to be turned ashore or eaten. If you wish, your mess
may have him for dinner, say on the holiday."

Barbe glared at me in astonishment, almost in horror,
as if I had suggested he was a steamboat sailor and not a
man-of-war's man born and bred; and then, recoiling as
Dick Dead-eye does in the play, he said, mournfully:

"Why, sir, I'd as soon eat my brother as that pig, as
that Dennis, sir! He's weathered o' all we have, and I'd
as leave stick my knife into a babby as into that animal.
Of course, sir, if it's go ashore, go it is, sir; but I'd like to
make terms with the man that's to have him, so Dennis
'll get the treatment and kindness he larned with us, sir."

It was as I had expected, and so the arrangements for
his new home were made at once.

Eheu, fugaces! Dennis went ashore the next day in
the dingy, bag and hammock, ribbons, dhudeen and potato and all, the men clustering in the bridle-ports and
gangways to salute him, and the officers waving a farewell
from aft. As his pigship pulled under the bows I heard
from forward a rousing cheer, and this was the last ship
greeting he was ever to know.

A countryman of ours had drifted into that land, and
Dennis had been consigned to his care under a guarantee that his later days should be spent on a plantation

inland, and that his sphere of duty should be as a breeder, for, doubly blessed, we had in Dennis a prize in pig strain we never knew.

I drifted ashore next day, and there, lying in the shadow of a pandanus near the beach shingle, his nose buried in his fore-trotters and his eyes closed in weary waiting and sorrow, was Dennis. He looked up mournfully as I entered the ship-chandler's, and gave me a grunt of sullen recognition, as if he felt I were the author of his misery, or, at least, an aider and abettor of those who had sent him into exile. His new owner said he had moped from the beginning, at first wistfully roaming about, and at last settling into the morbid melancholy condition in which I found him.

It happened fortunately to be liberty week for the men, and while we were discussing his woes the voices of some of our crew came from the landing. The transition was marvellous. Dennis sprang to his feet, gazed inquiringly seaward for a moment, and then, as the men's voices grew nearer and louder, he twisted his tail into the rigidity of a corkscrew and bounded beachward, where the liberty party was skylarking by the jetty under the palm-trees.

No need to describe the meeting nor the subsequent orgies. Dennis followed each party that came ashore, trotting after the men into the back country, sleeping in the bush, eating with them, and, it is reported, getting as drunk as they did. He was first at the beach to welcome the coming, the last to speed the going, filling his part of host with a grace and a dignity in town, and an abandon and a freedom in the country, that woke in after-days the tender regrets of his companions.

The dissipation of Dennis and his friends lasted a scant week, and when the last boat-load left the beach he

DENNIS O' KERRY

turned mournfully shoreward, unheeding the re-echoing
cheers they gave him, and staggered, swaying port and
starboard, blear-eyed and shaky, towards the loneliness of
his new home. He fell into gloomy ways; he lost his fat
and dignity; he seemed on the verge of a decline; he
took himself seriously as a persecuted exile in a far land.
Finally it was thought best to send him afield to his new
labors, and his master tried to woo him countryward, but
in vain. He had won his way into this American's heart,
for when force was suggested he declined to tie the pig's
legs together and throw him into a cart, as he would have
done with a pig of less degree. He declared that Dennis
was a gentleman by instinct, a little low in his mind just
then, but still a gentleman, and that he could wait until
Dennis might, as if in the gayety of a holiday, idly stray
with him in some early morning to the plantation inland.
But Dennis was obdurate and never gay, and so the day
before the ship sailed for Apia his old master (the ship's
cook) and the boatswain's mate were sent to him, for it
was known he would follow the trill of the bosun's call.
When he heard the familiar voices and saw the blue
shirts of his shipmates and caught the bird-like whistle of
the mate, he jumped to his feet, gave an ecstatic grunt,
and ran among the trees wildly, with the fire of youth
rioting in his trotters.

A two-wheeled cart was brought to the door, the driver
took the reins, the blue-jackets seated themselves in the
stern-sheets, and, with Dennis trotting gayly at the tail-
board, the merry companions waved a farewell to me as
they went slowly down the Purumu Road into the heart
of the land.

Just beyond the last police-station of the town a native bar-room faced the little curve where two roads
joined. Here the men dismounted, and here, after the

sailor fashion, they toasted their happy meeting in a drink, which Dennis shared; and then, mounting again, they rounded the bend where the eager shrubbery found the archway of the trees, and Dennis passed hillward out of my life forever.